THE CURRACH AND THE CORNCRAKE

A Novel

E. PIOTROWICZ

RESOURCE *Publications* • Eugene, Oregon

THE CURRACH AND THE CORNCRAKE
A Novel

Resource Publications
An Imprint of Wipf and Stock Publishers
199 W. 8th Ave., Suite 3
Eugene, OR 97401

www.wipfandstock.com

PAPERBACK ISBN: 979-8-3852-0651-3
HARDCOVER ISBN: 979-8-3852-0652-0
EBOOK ISBN: 979-8-3852-0653-7

VERSION NUMBER 01/29/24

FOR MY FATHER, MY SON, AND THE FATHER OF MY SON.

CONTENTS

The hero of this tale is not based on any one real or mythic person, and the island of Thréig exists only in these pages. Any resemblance to persons living or dead is coincidental. While containing echoes of myth, legend, and ancient history, this tale is completely fictional—which means, of course, that it's mostly true.

PART I

The Fisherman,
the Mermaid, and the Boy

1

H E BURIED HER IN the garden. The new parish priest rowed out from the mainland to read the rite of committal over her and was the only witness to the end of the old fisherman's blessed contentment, buried along with his wife of forty-five years. Most of the parish was either too feeble or too fearful to journey over the rough autumnal waters to the island. The cottage, perched as it was on the western cliff of Thréig, well off any main track, was not easily accessible to any but the most determined visitor. The parishioners had paid their respects at the funeral mass for *her* sake, leaving only the young priest to bless the ground under the rose bush by the dry-stone wall at the boundary between the garden and the sea cliff, which would be her final resting place.

But the souls of the just are in the hand of God, and no torment shall touch them.

He buried her in the garden. Like a seed, he planted her next to the rose bush, yet knowing that spring would bring no flower. Her dying had been long. The slow degeneration of balance, muscle, bone, and that vital organ of hope, without which none can survive. In his clear, youthful tenor, the new parish priest sang out words which held small meaning for him—words that take experience of living and encountering many loves and many deaths to fully grasp.

On this mountain he will destroy the veil that veils all peoples, the web that is woven over all nations; he will destroy death forever.

He buried her in the garden. Even as the wind rose with a moan and a rattle of the gate latch, bringing with it spray from the churning waves, and memories of quiet teatimes by the fire, with the raging storm without, and safety and warmth within, when words were needless, and silence was full as the sea. He buried over half a lifetime with her, and so in burying her

in the garden, he buried most of himself as well, as the young priest's voice rang on like a bell through the fog, those words that the young can't feel:

My soul is deprived of peace, I have forgotten what happiness is; I tell myself my future is lost, all that I hoped for from the LORD.

Everyone young and ambitious had left the island one by one for the mainland for jobs in cities and larger towns, pursuing enterprises of great pitch and moment, swept along the current of social change. The old and the stubborn had grown fearful of their growing isolation and, one by one, they too had pulled up roots, transplanting themselves in the nearest main-land village to die in the company of others—others whose memories and language brought the comfort of understanding. The young fled to bigger things: the promise of better money to be had and the elusive specter of opportunity. Now one of the only young men left even in the village itself was this new bare-faced priest with whom the twilight-folk of the parish felt awkward at Confession. *Like confessing to a child,* they would say of Father Martin. *What can he know of the soul and its struggles at his age?* Still, the young priest stood with Seán, the last small boat fisherman still resid-ing through all the seasons on Thréig, reading the psalms in his clear and vigorous tenor:

Precious in the sight of the Lord is the death of his faithful ones.

Precious the death. Precious the life. That precious life now extin-guished and planted next to the rose bush, still waiting. A life and a death of waiting. What did a young man know of affliction? The grief for loss, the relief for ended suffering, the guilt for surviving, and for not having done better. Cared better. Spoken better. Loved better. And the waiting—the *waiting*. Still, the young priest counseled Seán in his grief, or tried, as the old fisherman shoveled the damp black soil over his bride.

"Will you be giving up the old cottage, then? Going to Dublin to live with your boy?"

"Dublin? No, no . . . I'd just be in his way there. He's a busy man, as you can see. Too busy even for his mother's burial."

"Well, it's a long journey at short notice, to be sure. Understandable, though I'm sorry you haven't got him here with you in your time of need."

"Need? Nay, Father, there's no need. It was a long time that Muire-ann was ill. A long time to prepare myself for living on my own. Years will teach you that the hardest times are faced alone," the old man gestured to the empty kitchen garden as the wind came keening mournfully across the weather-beaten grass and boggy hills beyond the dry-stone wall.

"Perhaps if you moved to town. What a lonely, desolate place Thréig is now that you're on your own out here. Our good God, in His wisdom, said in the beginning that it's not good for a man to be alone. There's no need to keep yourself to yourself like this, especially when there's a community—people who knew you both before. They won't always fear you, you know. It could be a great comfort to hear the voices of other people around you again."

Seán's face contorted in a grimace that the priest took to be a pang of grief but came closer to visceral dread—dread of the voices; dread of the eyes that would look without trying to seem obvious; dread of the things *not* said as much as those feeble murmurs of condolence. He rubbed his forehead, wiping away the grimace along with the drops of perspiration.

"Thank you, Father. Thank you for your time, for the psalms, for coming all this way and taking all this trouble. I won't leave her even now she's gone. There's no call to leave what I've always known. And what would I do on the mainland, anyway? I'm an islander, born and bred. I'm used to quiet and solitude. Even when I shared this island with others, I looked for it. I've been a fisherman since my boyhood. My end is bound to be here in my home, overlooking the sea, with my Muireann waiting for me in the garden, not on a sickbed in town, watched and worried over by people who fear my words, just waiting for me to die. No, I've lived on the edge of the sea since my birth. I'll die here by the sea or in its throat."

Seán wiped his hands on a handkerchief and straightened the flat cap that hid his thinning gray hair. He turned half away and struck a match, holding it to the bowl of his pipe. He did so intending to be a bit rude to the young priest who didn't smoke. Not too rude. He could never be truly rude to a man of the cloth, regardless of how new that cloth was, but he wanted the young man gone from his island all the same and sought to drive him gently away.

"I'd ask you in for a whiskey, Father, if I didn't know you needed to get back for Vespers soon."

"Well now, that's kind of you, Seán. Another time, I hope. Come and see me, will you? The next time you're in town. Come and have a cup of tea with me and let me know how you're getting along."

"I will so, Father."

"And remember, my son, take your troubles and tears straight to the Lord in prayer. He comforts the broken-hearted." The young priest awkwardly patted Seán's shoulder with a mild expression of studied and terrible

sweetness, turned, and began hiking down toward the dirt path and the crisp blue and white rowboat that waited for him at the pier. Seán didn't watch him leave but hung up his spade and trudged inside the whitewashed cottage to his chair by the fire.

The evening was damp and chill. Seán poked the smoldering caorán in the grate and piled the glowing embers with cut peat from the creel. He propped up his feet by the warm glow and poured himself two fingers of whiskey. He winced at the first burning sip. A strong spirit for a strong sadness. It offered a warmth, however fleeting, to the iciness that ran through him.

"Well, Muireann—what am I to do now?" he asked the empty chair across from his, but the chair did not reply.

2

"She was alone. The floodwaters had taken all her kinsmen, but she endured, preserved in a cave below the water, though trapped. She sat huddled in a corner, the sharp edges of the rock walls catching and snagging at her clothing and leaving red, sandy dents in her pale skin.

"She was alone. Alone and afraid, contained within this watery barrier as though trapped inside a bubble and waiting—watching—in the long, silent hours, the long, slanting beams of light as they filtered through the surface of the water, all greens and blues and speckled with plankton as with billions of stars. She saw forms that seemed alive, not passive as drifting seaweed, but animated. She thought it was her imagination filling the void with shapes. She watched them come and go like the shadows that fell when clouds passed in front of the sun. Sometimes they were near, almost near enough to make out faces and eyes, yet she was not afraid. To the desperately lonely, any face is a welcome sight, even the one you only think you see.

"Her eyes became accustomed to the cave's darkness beneath the waters, and the shapes and forms continued to grow clearer. They came closer and closer to the edge of her watery cell, as curious of her as she was of them. They shimmered, long and sleek and graceful. 'How I wish I were one of them,' she sighed aloud. 'How I wish I were a salmon so that I would not be alone.'

"The goddess Danu heard her wish and granted it but halfway, making her half woman and half salmon—the Mermaid Lí Ban. Happily did she swim with the salmon. For three hundred years, she played with them in the waves and foam that churned in the coves and reefs. In the open waters she befriended the wisest and oldest whales, all crusted over in barnacles, watchful of the world, and singing, always singing the lore of their kind into the fathomless depths. Deep into midnight murk did she dive to see

9

the creatures with faces fierce, wild, and strange to the landsman, but which bear within themselves a light of their own making. She rode the swirling eddies and currents around far distant islands laughing, for she was no longer alone in this great teeming universe of the sea. Perhaps she would be there still today if not for the Fisherman and the Saint.

"I saw her shining head bob up and down like a seal amid the waves that swept in and out of the cove. I was baiting lobster creels. I'd rarely seen a swimmer in that cove before, let alone so fanciful a creature. I knew at once she was a mermaid, even though I had never seen one before. Her hair streamed out behind her like long, black seaweed, and her skin was white like the sea-caps. I thought to myself, *who is this magical creature swimming in my cove?* Do you know who she was, boy?"

"It was Mammy!"

"That's right! But she wasn't anybody's mammy then, nor anybody's bride. She was just a wild wisp of a girl washed up on my shore like a sparkling bit of seafoam. Beautiful. Beautiful like nothing and no one I'd seen in my life before."

"But she wasn't *really* a mermaid at all, or a bit of sea foam."

"No, but like Lí Ban, she was lonely and took to the waves to quench that loneliness that had dried her throat to aching. Her father had come for the summer fishing in one of the big boats, and left her to explore the island, just a wild motherless creature. I laid down my work and I scrabbled down the rocks—"

"In your bare feet!"

"—in my bare feet, and do you know what she said to me? This wild mermaid girl?"

"She said, 'what are you doing fishing in my cove, you bloodthirsty child?'"

"And I said to her—"

"'*Child* is it? I'm clearly some years older than you!'"

"And she repeated herself, trying not to laugh—"

"'What are you doing fishing in my cove?'"

"And I holler to her, laughing—"

"'What are you doing swimming in *mine*?'"

"We both laughed then and decided that the only fair thing was to share it between us. We met there every day after that, the whole summer long, when I'd finished my work and was free to play, though I'd thought up till then that I was too old for playing. Oh, those long summer days! I

would lay down my nets and gear and lobster creels, and we would swim together in the cove, pretending. That was her game. Always pretending. She was always playing out the old stories like they were true, and we were the ones who did the heroic deeds. We made the old stories true by living them together."

"And you fell in love."

"We fell in love, but she left at summer's end with her father, following the migrant laborers up into the Hebrides, following the work. I thought my tender young heart would break. I spent the lonely, gray months that followed doubting I'd ever seen her at all. Doubting we'd had that summer of playing pretend. Doubting I'd swum with a mermaid."

"But she came back!"

"She did. Every summer, she came back, and every summer she was less of a girl and more of a woman, until the summer her father left for good. But this time she stayed behind, for I had caught her in my net and carried my mermaid laughing to shore, as in the old story. She let me catch her, for she was not willing again to leave me and our island or the cove we shared. I held her in my arms and kissed her wet, dripping seaweed hair, kissed her eyelids, and her mouth that seemed always ready to smile and brimmed with the sweetest laughter. I held her in my arms and wouldn't let her go, though, to be sure, she never tried.

"She took to land and taught the island children at the very school you walk to for your lessons. I would walk to the schoolhouse to find her every day after the children had left, and together we would walk hand in hand in the salty breeze, looking out not toward Errigal and the mainland but out toward the sea. We talked and talked of voyages, of ancient saints and heroes and monsters, but we talked most of all about the day we would marry. And we *did* marry. I built this cottage right here on the cliff above the place where we first met, so my mermaid should never have to leave her cove."

"And then *I* was born!"

"And then you were born, Callum, though we thought we'd never see the day."

"I was a miracle!"

"A miracle, to be sure. We thought we'd be childless forever. Many's the tear we shed in the waiting. But then you came . . . "

"On a foggy morning!"

"When we'd long given up hope and waiting. A miraculous child indeed. Then our joy was—"

"Complete!"

"You've heard this story so many times you can tell it to me when I'm old, and my memories have ebbed with the tide!"

"Then the simple fisherman, the mermaid, and their boy—"

"Lived happily ever after, cozy on that island cliff, safe from the raging of the sea."

* * *

"Muireann, my mermaid, can you hear me?" Seán spoke again to the empty chair across from his. "What am I to *do* now? Happily ever after . . . but you've both gone and left me on this rock alone." He sat in his own patched armchair, waiting. *Waiting.* The old mantle clock marked the lonely seconds mercilessly with each hard, hollow *tock.* He sipped again at the whiskey, which burnt him less than before, and watched the orange embers heaving and sighing like a tiny dozing dragon in the grate.

How had the story gone? The one about the mermaid? She had come to live on land, was baptized by a saint, and became human. She lived with her simple fisherman quietly, happily in that whitewashed stone cottage on the salt-blasted cliff. By that very dozing fire, she had told him stories. Stories of peril and adventure, of heroes and saints—stories she'd heard in her migratory flight from port to port, blending and mixing them with reality until they seemed one and the same. The ancient stories in the ancient tongue, punctuated always with the refrain: *Oul fellas are meant to rove about, not sit like a wrinkled old spud in the cellar 'till what eyes they have see nothing.* Always she said it, no matter the story. He'd laughed, though he'd never completely understood what she meant by it.

"What did it mean, Muireann? What does it mean?" He spoke to the empty chair where his mermaid once had sat, nursing their child, mending the ruptured knees of his trousers, singing those old songs in the old tongue, and telling those old tales. The tales of Saint Columcille were her favorites because he felt so close. *He was born near here. Not far at all. Can you imagine that great saint standing in our cove? Perhaps he rowed himself out to our island. Perhaps he saw angels here, on that very rock where you sit on mild summer evenings with your pipe. But he had to leave his homeland. So might you one day. May it be for adventure rather than exile—though maybe the two aren't so very different after all.*

"I don't understand, Muireann. I don't understand what I'm to do now without my mermaid and her stories. Without our boy—our Callum—our own small Columcille. How you loved the name. You thought he'd be a saint too, found a monastery here on Thréig, see the angels and insult the demons. Become part of the legends himself. Perhaps you wanted it too much. You waited for him, but now you're both gone, and *I'm* the one waiting. My darling, what am I to do with myself while I wait?"

Oul fellas are meant to rove about, she used to say, without caring to say what she meant by it.

"I should have cared for you better from the start. Maybe then you wouldn't have taken ill. Maybe I'd still have you. Three *years* in your bed. Three *years*, when my mermaid couldn't go down to the water. Couldn't swim in the waves and laugh like the seabirds on the cliff. Three *years* of my poor cooking, until you couldn't eat at all. I'd always imagined you returning to sea foam when your time came. But, in spite of our playing at myths and legends, you weren't really a mermaid after all. You were a sick woman, and I was your poor caretaker. You deserved better, my darling girl. But who will I care for now? What am I to do?"

Oul fellas are meant to rove about, she used to say, as though it were terribly important.

"But there's nothing left to explore," Seán said to the empty chair. "There's nothing out there that I want to see anymore. I'd like to see our boy—our Callum's a man now with a life that I know nothing about. He could be married with children of his own, and I wouldn't know. How I do wish to see him, but I fear he'll not see me after everything. Why should he want to see *me*? Anyway, he's educated and distinguished and important now. I'm everything he didn't want to be, except the saint you prayed he'd be. Don't think I wasn't aware that your dream was for us both—your boys. But you can't force sainthood on a person. No matter how you pray and pour your wise words into him like holy water. It was always too late for me. The saints were learned men and women—learned in the deep things. The deepest thing I've ever known is the sea. And we both know that's not as deep as you wanted us to go. Now I'm old—old and tired and alone on an island where no one else wants to be anymore. What am I to do?"

Oul fellas are meant to rove about, she had said in her weak and wobbling voice, grown quiet and unsteady over the waning years of her illness, when her eyes had grown cavernous—her cheekbones high and sharp—her skin like crinkled paper, yellowed and pale.

"Muireann! Muireann! We should have had more time to explore *together*, you and me. I was never meant to outlive you! I never built you that boat I promised you when we used to look out to sea and talk about the holy islands where sinners became saints! The sailing ship! I never took you to Iona! You knew all the stories, and yet I never took you to see Saint Columcille's island. Now it's too late."

Oul fellas are meant to rove about, she'd said, her weak, bony hand clutching his from under the quilt, as though, of all the things a dying woman could tell the man she left behind, this was the most important.

"Not without you, Muireann! Not without my mermaid. What would be the point of it? What is the point of my life now at all? My life was you— you and our Callum. The life we made here for ourselves. What could I find out there to make up for all that I've lost? What if all my roving about only brings me back to this grief—grief for the ways I failed you. To be sure, it's young men who have the right to explore. Young men with their lives ahead of them and everything to gain. There's nothing more for me. I've spent it all and wasted more than I'll ever know."

Oul fellas are meant to rove about, she'd said, as she closed her eyes for the last time, the heaving of her ribcage slowing and becoming more and more shallow with the ebbing of life, like the tide pulling away from the rocky shore.

The peat fire was dying, and a drilling white rain broke through the sky with a crash and a blasting wind. Seán had felt the storm before it came. Felt it in his knees and hips. "I'm old. Too old to rove about. Too old to explore. Too old to leave my fireside and my chair. Too old to go without my tea. Too old to bear the storm's blast when the wind rises, and out of nowhere, the sea transforms from kitten to tiger. Too old. I'm too old to venture beyond the cove, the rocks and tides and currents and safe harbors I've known all my life. I'm too old. There's nothing left for me but to join you in the garden when the Lord sees fit to close my eyes, whether here in my chair or in my boat down in the cove. I'm just too old."

3

"ONCE UPON A TIME, some 1300 years ago, there lived a man and a woman, both of noble birth and lineage. Their names were Fedhlimidh and Eithne. One day, Eithne was given the gift of a divine vision. She saw a most beautiful veil, fine and shimmering, scattered with the most delicate boughs and fronds and golden flowers of paradise. She reached out her hand to touch it, but as she did so, it fluttered away upwards as though caught on a sudden breeze. She wept when it disappeared from her view entirely, for it was the most beautiful veil surpassing any she had ever seen, and she was a daughter of kings accustomed to the finest things. But as she wept and grieved its loss, an angel of strange and unspeakable beauty, clad in light, came to her and spoke: 'Do not grieve for the veil. Truly it was but a sign of the child you shall bear.'

"Eithne went at once to her husband Fedhlimidh and told him of her vision and of the angel's words. He expanded with pride, for he believed it was a sign that his child would be like the heroes of old, a fierce warrior, brave and strong, in the line of the Hy-Nialls. But owing to the gentleness of the vision, his mother doubted her husband's interpretation and invited him to see the portent differently; that the nature of this vision and the angel's message seemed to foretell a spiritual or prophetic greatness. This they both finally agreed, and when the child was born, they had him christened with the name Columcille, meaning 'Dove of the Church,' in keeping with their belief in his high spiritual calling.

"This darling child ran the fields and beaches just as you do, climbed the sea cliffs in search of speckled birds' eggs, and for the fun of feeling as though he, himself, were flying over the sea. He was born not far from here, you know. He climbed the cliffs in his bare feet just as you do and gazed at the tide pools and their gardens of colorful anemones, urchins, and crabs. He watched the storm petrels, gannets, and gulls that sliced the air, and he

swam in the frigid waves. Perhaps he collected the cowries and smooth tumbled stones that he found on the shore, just as you do.

"Now, when young Columcille was the proper age, he left behind his playing with the shorebirds and shells, and he went away to learn. Custom dictated that the sons of chiefs be brought up from their youth by some great master of whatever trade they were intended—a soldier, a bard, or a priest. So young Columcille went to be raised by the old holy priest, Cruithnechan, who had administered the sacred rites of baptism and chrismation to him as a babe.

"Happily did young Columcille live and learn in the Church. Before the boy could read, he was memorizing the Psalms and took delight in the chanting of the Divine Office. One day, saintly Cruithnechan lost his place in the Psalter and became distressed that he could not find it and was hindering the prayers of the faithful. But Columcille's sweet, angelic voice rang out the continuation of the Psalm by heart until his spiritual father could find his place again.

"You see, Saint Columcille loved the Church from boyhood and often nestled quietly by the altar while the other boys played rowdy games outside or focused their attentions on more worldly things. But in spite of all his gentle love for the Church and the Psalms, young Columcille was still a Hy-Niall by blood, and that hot blood could at times make him haughty and slow to forgive. You see, my sweet boy, even Saint Columcille had his cross to bear. But despite all that, he learned well from old Cruithnechan, and by the time he was of age, Columcille had learned all that the holy man had to teach of lore both heroic and saintly, earthly and heavenly."

Callum's eyelids grew heavy as he sat on the cottage floor by the fire listening to his mother's low, smooth voice, warm and golden like summer sunshine, as she told him the story of his patron saint again. He watched the peat fire and leaned his head against his mother's knee. His mind swam with images of a young boy, much like himself, yet different. For *he* didn't know the Psalms and learning anything by heart was difficult. He couldn't have helped old Cruithnechan when he lost his place in the Divine Offices, and he would rather have been collecting shells and stones than sitting quietly by the altar, heavy and drowsy with hovering clouds of sweet incense smoke. He was a boy who needed to move—needed to run and to climb and to work with his hands. He was the kind of boy who wanted to trace the pattern of a shell or squint hard to see the tiny hooks and barbules on a gannet's flight feather, locking and unlocking them like a zipper. The

kind of boy who wanted to experiment and find things out about the world around him. A thought had recently begun to tickle Callum at the back of his mind that perhaps he'd been named for the wrong saint. Was there not a saint who didn't care to read and memorize long passages of scripture? Perhaps a saint who preferred the wisdom of wild things to the wisdom of scholars? What if he had been given the wrong name?

Some boys are named after their fathers. Why was he not named after his? Was it wrong to be simple? To take out a boat and catch fish for your living and your supper? Surely even Jesus' disciples had their start mending nets and gutting fish. Callum shuddered, recalling the thunking stroke of the blade separating the fish from its head—the smear and smell on his clothes and the feeling of scales under his fingernails. Gulls hovering nearby like wastepaper caught on the breeze, waiting patiently for the guts and eyeballs that were going spare. No, perhaps it was right that he hadn't got his father's name. It filled him with shame to hold something in his hands, one moment squirming with life, but then to end that life with such swift practicality—one life after another. *Thunk. Slap. Thunk. Slap. Thunk.* He hated it all and wanted nothing of it. He was something in between or something else entirely. What name he ought to have had, Callum couldn't say. He wanted something for himself he'd never seen before—yearned for something he wasn't convinced existed. He wasn't sure what it was yet, but he would know it when he found it.

4

THE DAY CAME WET as Seán woke still in his chair where he'd fallen asleep to the wind-rattled creaks and patterings of the late September storm. The room was cold, though drenched in the rich, sad light of the autumn sunrise. The fire had long died out. He attempted to rise from his chair but found his legs to be stiff and sore from too long in the same position. He felt nearly paralyzed, not only because his heavy old legs didn't wish to hold him, but because he lacked the will to make them. He groaned in his chair, rubbing the muscles of his thighs with gnarled old hands.

"You see, Muireann? Too old! My legs don't even work! And how am I to go out adventuring and exploring when I can't even get out of my chair in the morning?" He gripped the back of his neck with a grimace. "And that hurts as well. The only thing that doesn't hurt me is my stomach. I suppose it'll start soon enough if I don't get my oats." And yet the old man stayed in his chair, rubbing his neck, his legs, the small of his back and looking scornfully at the empty chair across from his. "Well, there's one consolation, at least. I'll not have to wait long for the Cóiste Bodhar to come swinging round the corner. The way I feel this morning, I'd wager it's just down the hill and coming fast. No, I'll not give old Dullahan the courtesy of coming down to meet him. Let those ghostly horses of his do the hard work and get him up here on their own." Seán folded his arms across his chest and pulled his cap down over his face. "Let him come. I'll not stop him. I'll not rush out to meet him, but I'll not stop him."

A quarter of an hour passed by and as predicted, Seán's empty stomach began to churn. "Damnation! Why can't an old man die in peace!" He punched a bony fist at his middle as though that might stop its growling. "Fine! Fine! I suppose old Dullahan might like a cup of tea when he arrives anyway, though I'd like to see him try and drink it without a head." Seán heaved himself out of his chair, built up the fire, and filled the kettle. "And

what's a cup of tea without a bit of porridge? That's right—eat up, old man. You'll likely be dead by evening." He cast a glance over at the chair across from his. "Now don't you be looking at me like that, Muireann, you know it's true. I'm old and I'm ready! . . . soon as I've had a bite to eat."

Seán mixed the oats into the bubbling water, watching them roil and toss like debris from a wrecked ship crashing in foam along the shoreline. He stirred absentmindedly, scraping his spoon across the bottom of the pot, then left it simmering to fetch two bowls from the cupboard. Spooning the oats into the first bowl, his hand paused trembling over the second. "Damnation!" He cursed under his breath, his eyes growing foggy with the threat of tears. Seán returned the second bowl to the cupboard and heaped the first bowl to the brim with two servings of porridge.

With a cup of tea in him, and more porridge than he had wanted, Seán reckoned it wouldn't hurt to wash up a bit. After all, if death was coming, at least the priest would find him clean when he came to fetch his remains. The practice would do that boy-priest some good. A few more deaths, a few more mourners, funeral masses, and burials. Maybe losing someone dear of his own and he'd be able to read those Psalms with that tremulous, meaningful quality that old priests have, for they actually know what it is they're saying.

Seán grumbled as he scrubbed himself over the washbasin, scowling over at the bedroom door that he didn't dare open. No, he would never open it again if he could avoid it. That was the room where she'd died, and he couldn't face its emptiness.

He supposed it did feel better to be clean and full of breakfast, and a walk down the cove certainly wouldn't hurt him. Maybe his legs would feel a bit livelier, not that it mattered if they did or not. He wasn't long for this world, after all, and malfunctions of the body didn't merit any kind of special treatment. He picked his way down the rocky cliff to a little sandy stretch of beach. He stood looking from that spot out at their cove, but that only made him think of her, and the last time she'd made the climb down to this spot.

She shouldn't have done it, to begin with. That was only the beginning of her trouble, though the true beginning was hard to place in time. Perhaps it had started long before, but neither of them had noticed, or perhaps she just hadn't complained. She never was one to draw attention to her own pain, and it frightened Seán to think how long she might have suffered silently for fear of troubling him. Perhaps she had known her end

was beginning, but Seán had not, or at least hadn't accepted it until the end of the end drew near. She'd been feeling "a little poorly" for a long while and thought a bracing swim in the cold water might liven her limbs and her lungs. She had always been a strong swimmer, and it was when he had to rescue her that day that he realized hers was more than a trifling illness.

Muireann had no reason to think she'd gone out too far, and it came upon her unexpectedly. She hadn't the strength or the breath to swim back to shore, and the currents were pulling her under. Seán had been out in the boat pulling up lobster creels not far from shore when he heard the splashing and the frantic cries, *like a banshee*, he'd thought at the time, and scarcely less portentous. He'd dived in after her and pulled her, exhausted, to shore. The fear in her eyes had been terrible to behold—a look he'd never seen in them before. She had known, as now did he, that her illness was more serious than it had seemed, and she no longer had the strength they'd both taken for granted all those years. They'd sat on the boulder, and he had grasped her, almost crushed her to his chest, in his frantic fear of losing her. She had struggled to catch her breath. He'd kissed her wet and draggled hair, no longer black, but fully silver—kissed her weeping eyelids, kissed her mouth, no longer laughing, but down-turned and trembling with cold and fear. Like kissing a skull, he had thought at the time. Like kissing death or the fear of it.

Seán now sat on that same boulder down in the cove and stared out at the waves that had almost taken her that day. Perhaps it would have been better if they *had* taken her, rather than to face the next three years of slow and painful decline. He squeezed shut his eyes, bowing his head in guilt for even thinking such a thing. Surely there had been moments, precious ones, within those three years that he would not wish to have missed. But he loved her, and her suffering had gutted him like a fish, and left him feeling just as empty and helpless.

Seán had carried her over his shoulder that day—the day she'd almost drowned—not like he had done when they were young and playing at legends of fishermen and mermaids. Not easily, and with laughter, but with great effort and an aching heart, up the steep cliff and granite boulders to the cottage draped over his shoulder. He'd carried her for she hadn't a shred of strength left in her to get back up from the shore. That was the day he became more than a fisherman. He became a nursemaid, a cook, a housekeeper, at first only on her bad days, until all of her days were bad.

Those years had finally taught him the full meaning of what it meant to be a husband . . . but now what was he?

His grief perched heavy and painful on his shoulder, like a huge cormorant from the other, darker, side of being. Its wings spread wide at its sides, arching inward, around him, darkening the edges of everything. It juddered and hissed in his ear, as they do when angered, picking and prying greedily at the edges of every fond memory, turning them over and over until they, too, were tainted with regret, swallowed slowly down the creature's long, dark, snake-like throat.

Seán propped one elbow on his knee to rest his chin in his hand. He stared at the churning, boiling waves smashing themselves relentlessly against the rocks. Why had Callum not come? Whatever the boy held against *him*, he had dearly loved his mother. Why had he not come to help bury her at least? Come to mourn with his father?

Seán had written letters. Written them when he felt the end was not far off. He thought their boy would want to say goodbye to his mother. Why hadn't he come? Not even a response to say he was too busy. Nothing. Surely Seán had let the boy down in many ways that he would never understand—let slip words of potency and power he hadn't intended—but was that sufficient reason to abandon his mother in her final days?

Those final days . . . days that dragged, slow and painful. Waiting. Waiting for Callum. Waiting for death. Waiting for that last long dissonant chord to resolve, fade, and put an end to the slow dirge that had defined the past three years. And here he was now sitting on their rock at the end of the song, in the silence following the last note, stripped bare of everything that he had been, and left only with feelings he couldn't bear. Waiting.

Seán stared out at the waves. The crescendo of their rushing in and fading back in ripples of white foam lulled him into a sort of vacancy of mind where his pain and grief felt duller and more distant, like the great cormorant had released its grip and now hovering dark-winged just over his shoulder, but no longer pressing on him the fullness of its weight. As he watched the waves come and go, the light on the surface of the water changed from the thick slanting autumnal hue of the season to a younger, thinner, purer light that sparkled on the waves. Summer light. He looked down at his strong, smooth young hands, deftly baiting the lobster creel with mackerel offal. He smiled and raised his eyes back to the sparkling water, knowing that the waves would soon bring him a laughing girl with long dripping ropes of black hair. This time he wouldn't hesitate. He wouldn't

wait. He had waited enough in his life. This time he would dive into the waves, forsaking his work, and swim with her there in the cove.

Seán watched with shallow breath and waited until a shining dark head rose shyly from the gentle summer waves, but he found he couldn't move to join her. His body was frozen there on the rock, and the timid bobbing head ducked down under the waves with a chuckling splash, disappearing from view. His body tensed and jerked with the effort to rise and chase after her, until he began to ache all over with cold. His feet and ankles were wet with the rising tide. A harbor seal stared at him through round, filmy eyes, nostrils flaring, its shining black head rising from the autumn churn of the sea.

5

"AFTER LEAVING WISE OLD Cruithnechan, our young Saint Columcille served as a deacon under none other than Saint Finnian of Movilla. Now, Saint Finnian once set out upon the sea from the Irish shores to visit Rome—a perilous journey. You see, in those days, the currach he set out in would have been little more than a twisting of thin, supple boughs for a frame with ox skins stretched over it like a drum. Besides the vulnerability of his ship, the seas were dangerous in those days, not only for the famine, pestilence, and illness one faces on long sea voyages, but for the Vikings and pirates marauding about the coasts."

"Pirates!"

"And Vikings. Saint Finnian's poor currach could have been easily destroyed by such dangerous and desperate men as these, but miraculously, he arrived at Rome and stayed there seven years. He came back ordained as a priest but bore with him one other gift even more precious than his own Holy Orders."

"What was it?"

"It was the Holy Scriptures, Callum."

"The Holy Scriptures? But they aren't so special. We have that book just there, on the stand. You read to us from it every day. Everyone has that book, Mammy."

"Yes, well, it may not be so unusual a thing today, but back in those days, books of any kind were rare and precious things, written all by hand on leaves of vellum, and this book was a treasure! This was the first book of the Holy Scriptures to abide in our lands, and our dear Saint Columcille would have seen it! Touched it! Read it!"

"Is that the one he copied?"

"You're skipping ahead, Callum."

Callum scratched his tussled head and stared over at the family Bible on its stand. He couldn't imagine a world without books in it, or for that matter a world in which a book might be one's greatest treasure. He himself had a box of treasures he kept hidden under his bed, and none of them were books. A remnant of shell from a kittiwake's egg. Colorful bits of sea glass. A few smooth cowries and bivalve fossils. The partial skull of a guillemot, its braincase, one intact eye-socket, and still-sharp beak. The greatest, and largest of his treasures, though, was a sperm whale's tooth.

"Do you think the whale that swallowed up Jonah had teeth like this?"

Callum's questions about the Holy Scriptures were rarely of a spiritual nature. But old bones filled him with a peculiar fascination that nothing else on earth could. To him, they prophesied. Those old bones whispered and chattered not only of the past, but of what was bound to come, and that filled him with fear, for he knew what was coming would be difficult—painful even, as the wave that smashes and drags you against the rock face. It occurred to Callum that, like Saint Columcille, he had been granted a vision, but he did not like what he'd seen.

Oftentimes Callum would lie in his bed holding this precious whale's tooth in his hands, clutched to his chest like some children might hold a well-loved toy. He had heard that some people carved them and etched pictures of ships and of mermaids into the ivory. Callum imagined what it would feel like, smell like, to spend three days in the belly of such a whale. Dark, slippery, and sour-smelling, he thought. He gripped the tooth more tightly thinking, not for the first time, and certainly not the last, that he should have been named after Jonah—not Columcille, who happily sequestered himself on a barren island praying and reading. Callum wanted to sail in the opposite direction of such a destiny.

* * *

The days dragged into weeks, and all passed in similar fashion for Seán. He would talk to Muireann's empty chair, sleep uneasily in his own, and cast scornful glares at the bedroom door until he couldn't bear to look at it at all. He woke painfully stiff each morning, a little surprised to find himself still alive. He would reluctantly drink down his cup of tea and eat his double portion of porridge (*damnation! he'd done it again!*) without pleasure. Then he would walk out into the kitchen garden, now withered brown and embalmed in October frost. He would rattle open the gate and climb down to

his boulder in the cove. There he would stare at the Atlantic as it seemed to rush eagerly into its seasonal changes, anticipating a long winter of gray squalls, lashing hale, and long, dark nights. He would stare at the waves until the darkness of his thoughts frightened him, and then climb back home to the cottage, to the door he wouldn't look at, and to his chair in front of the fire.

Seán had never moved a piece of furniture or changed the resting place of any item in the cottage, such a creature of habit had he become, until the day he could bear no longer to see the bedroom door even out of the corner of his eye. He turned his chair more squarely before the fire so that the door was fully to his back. That door. It was growing more loathsome to him with every passing day. That room he dared not enter or in any way disturb. It was too heavy with the memories of those last three years—those last breathless moments. He would live, and sleep and die in his chair rather than look at that empty bed again.

Seán lowered himself achingly into the chair and plumped a pillow to support his lower back. He propped up his feet to the embers and stared at them vaguely, testing the degree to which they felt real and present. He stared long and hard at his toes until they seemed something apart from him—just some bit of tackle dropped by the fire to dry. Yes, he was nearly ready.

It was after his double portion of oats, his double portion of grieving on the boulder in the cove, that he allowed himself this one abstract comfort, of which he'd discovered himself capable that first morning on the beach. That morning after burying Muireann. But he found it was more comfortably done in his chair, where the tide wouldn't find his feet as he lingered.

As Seán examined the toes that seemed no longer quite toes at all, he realized that nothing *was* what it *was* anymore. Everything was really something else. Something wordless and faint. His eyelids felt heavy and already the sound of his own breath surprised him in drifting gusts. His lids fell shut, and the fireplace, along with the feet that weren't really feet, began to melt. It all melted away like a fog and golden sunshine came leaking in the space that was left—just a small trickle of light at first that grew into the streaming rectangle of a doorway onto the sunny shore. He got up in that certain way he was only able to once his body had stiffened, paralyzed in the chair with shallow sleep, and went out into the timescape of otherwhere and of all-memory which existed beyond the vanished fire.

There in that rocky shore-like corridor—the place between deep sleep and waking where dreams were still malleable and memories could be visited—altered—improved, Seán breathed the damp dark-smelling air of his past. Despite the golden light of that placeless shore, the smell was of a cellar where things were kept preserved on shelves, where dust and cobwebs settled, and where old potatoes grew eyes. He moved forward, feeling for a corner that he might turn, leaning for a while into someplace comfortable. Yes, a comfortable memory was what he wanted. A place to linger for a while and rest his weary mind. He walked down the shore of other-where through every-time he'd ever lived until he felt a slight resistance, like a thin and sticky web, invisible yet impassible, that compelled him to turn. He pressed and squeezed himself into the narrow opening at the turning and flung himself into Muireann's embrace.

Muireann was crying, but not with sorrow. Her face was glowing, tired but radiant. The best day. He'd walked into the best day! Seán held the fragile wailing bundle in the crook of his arm as Muireann wrapped her arms around the both of them. He had never known such joy—such fear. It had felt back then as if the day would never come. They had thought it was too late for them—too late for her. All the parish had been surprised that the boy wouldn't bear his father's name. *His name is Callum* they both had said. For the nature of his birth, like Saint Columcille, seemed such a miracle as to portend to a spiritual greatness.

And as Seán held the babe in his arm, it grew. Time in the present feels eternal, but in that place of *every*-time—*all*-time—it came in rushes and halts like the tide. The little boy sat perched now in the crook of Seán's arm, like a falcon, looking at him through one eye, then the other, opening and closing his little mouth, not with speech or laughter or crying, but with a strange, hard clacking noise. But that wasn't right . . . Seán turned again toward Muireann, his mouth full of questions, but she was pale . . . gasping. Seán set the little boy down on the boulder and ran to pick up his wife's long, limp form. He rushed her into the waves, for she was drowning of air. He pushed her pale greenish face into the water so that she could breathe. She wasn't meant to turn so soon, back to her first body. She slipped from his fingers into the waves, though he tried so hard to hold on to her now writhing, scaly, legless form. It wasn't time! And anyway, he was older than her. Seán stared despairingly at the waves until her glossy head rose to the surface like a smooth, dark island, a thin, green finger trailing seaweed pointed, urged him to look back toward the shore. *The child!*

Seán whipped around to see Callum, growing larger, spreading his skinny little arms as if in benediction, perched there on the boulder. The flight feathers were now fully grown in and his face was darkening with feathery growth beyond recognition, but for the eyes that had passed from father to son. Seán lunged toward the boulder, feeling with every step—time—sea—sand—weed—all holding him back from reaching his boy. If only he hadn't set him down and looked away! Why had he looked away? Now he would lose them both—her to the sea—him to the sky! He strained at the thick oozing waves, bubbling like porridge around his legs, but seemed to move backward with every step in spite of his lunging and fling-ing. He reached and fought and tried to shout. No sound would come from his throat but a mute rasp of forced air, frantic and inarticulate as a fish struggling against the net. The boy now crouched, his head tucked down between those high shoulders, his eyes fixed on his father's, and sprang from the boulder into flight.

Seán fell backwards into the waves—falling down under the water—falling down the long silent corridor of *every*-where and *every*-time, its rocky corridors smearing around him as he plummeted into the dark va-cancy of *no*-where and *no*-time—sideways now as though time and himself with it were being poured from a bottle. He fell with a jolt into his chair. The hearth, the glowing peat, the feet that really were just feet reasserted themselves and Seán mopped the salty wetness from his face. It hadn't been comfortable for very long that time. It almost wasn't worth it if it was always going to end this way. He rose groaning with a crackling noise issuing from his knees and ankles and went to put the kettle on. The tea canister was bare.

6

I T WAS ONLY THE want to tea that led Seán finally to consider rowing that scant mile across to the mainland and wandering into town. How he had dreaded it. His breath was fast and shallow, but every deep breath he sucked in made his head swim and little sparks and dazzles swarm like midges at the edges of his vision. He was not on good terms with the folk in the village, and that was his own doing, he admitted that much. They had used to have friends there, but then, *he* had used to be different. He wasn't always as cold and stony as Muireann's last years had made him toward those who probably only wanted to help. But they were insufferable, those women, who had tried in every way possible to boss him and take over when Muireann was so ill.

Maeve, an incorrigible busybody, had cornered him in town one day and scolded him for keeping Muireann's care to himself. *It's indecent!* She'd shrilled at him like an angry seagull. *And what did a musty old fisherman like him know of nursing the ill! Why, Muireann was probably still poorly because he wouldn't take any help. He was a stubborn, stupid old man and she felt sorry for poor Muireann!* Her bunched up, self-righteous lips had sat pursed atop a wobbling stack of chins as she finished her speech, evidently satisfied that she had unburdened her conscience. Normally Seán would have shut his mind to Maeve's words, nodded amiably as if he hadn't heard them at all, and gone about his business, but that day he had lost his temper. It didn't happen often, but he supposed he'd been on the edge of it for a while, and the weight of all his fears and anger piling up on him over time finally made something break loose inside him. That was the day he had let fly such a curse that the angels in heaven would have cringed at its vileness. It was made even more terrifying by the oozing, sticky rage behind his unnaturally calm voice as he said it.

"May you die without a priest and may the gates of paradise never open to you! To hell with you, woman! To *hell* with you!" He recalled a long string of other saltier words that had passed his lips, which a man ought never to say to a woman, no matter how bossy she might be, or how may chins she may possess. He flung every curse he'd ever heard, even those concerning avenging orphans, stinging pismires, and man-eating cats. But it was that bit about death without a priest that would go down in local lore, since later that night Maeve *did* die of a stroke in her sleep, and Father Martin was, indeed, out of town at the time. When she was discovered lying expired in her bed, her old green-eyed cat was found staring menacingly from beside her head on the pillow. To think what other vile parts of Seán's curse might have come to be if Maeve hadn't been found when she was.

Word spread quickly that Seán had brought this death upon poor Maeve through his ill-timed and curiously specific malediction. Poor Maeve's bitter tongue and widespread interference in the affairs of others was swiftly glossed over, and her memory revised in a most saintly light. To be sure, she hadn't been interfering so much as *caring*, nor bitter so much as *honest*. A good woman, all things considered. A pillar of the community and an example to them all of Christian charity and virtue. Maeve had never been so beloved in life as she was in death.

The consensus within the community was that Seán—quiet, simple Seán who minded his own business and never said much—was secretly a practitioner of the black arts. *It's always the quiet ones, to be sure.* Only a few really thought that in earnest, but the rest kept their distance just to be safe. They had shown up to the funeral mass for Muireann's sake, not for his, and had given him only the most distant and cautious of condolences.

Frankly, Seán felt he deserved the shunning, and took it as his just punishment for his sins. Maybe not everyone believed he had practiced a dark bit of magic on Maeve, but *he did*, and his conscience bled for it. He feared seeing them all now that they avoided meeting his eyes, whispered, and crossed themselves when he passed.

The want of tea, however, is a powerful force. Finally, one chill bleak tealess morning in late October, Seán took out the old currach and fished in the early dawn. Having a decent haul, or decent enough, he slapped the fish into a large creel and rowed to the mainland. His head and back ached, not from his labor, but from the expectation of forthcoming fearful condolences when he showed up in town. The pained expressions of those who didn't know what to say, or thought they did, but would have done better

to say nothing; the imperious looks of those who thought Muireann might still be living had Seán allowed them to help…had he not been so damned stubborn and proud. Worst of all, he dreaded the frightened staring of those who thought he might curse them on a whim to some horrendous death. Still, if he was going to be living a bit longer, it was time he came to town and sold a few fish, bought some tea and other necessities, collected his mail, and paid young Father Martin that visit he'd promised.

* * *

"Those we love don't go away, they walk beside us every day, unseen, un-heard, but always near, still loved, still missed and very dear.' We do miss your Muireann. She was a queen among women!" Saoirse said as she took three pollack off him.

"Is—is that a Turbot?" Pat said as he fumbled with his cap in his hands, nervous of meeting Seán's eye and provoking an eloquent curse. "L-love me a good flat fish for Friday supper. I—I'll have it! No, no—it's certainly worth all that—I don't want any change!"

"Many of those who sleep in the dust of the earth shall awake; some shall live forever; others shall be in everlasting horror and disgrace . . . but surely your Muireann shall be like the stars forever—shining above us all. Though . . .perhaps she might have been with us a bit longer still, had . . . well, let's not talk of what might have been." Angela said, looking meaningly at Seán from the corner of her eye, for she fancied herself a bit of a witch herself with talents at healing with certain plants and herbs. She pretended to examine each fish, lifting them by the tales and giving them a little point-less waggle, but didn't buy one.

Seán responded simply with nods and grunts of thanks where it seemed right, and silence where it seemed wisest while pocketing more coins than expected for his morning's catch. When finally he had sold them all—all but the plump cod he'd reserved for Father Martin—he sat for a moment by the pier, commenting under his breath that it could have gone worse. "They'll not always trip over themselves trying to think what to say. They'll be over her in another week I daresay, and over their fear of me in another few weeks after that. I'll be glad when *they're* over it, though I suppose *I'll* never be." He cleared his throat and took out his pipe. As he reached for his pouch, a faint, thin cry came from underneath the skeleton of a derelict currach rotting down aways on the shore. A feeble weeping

cheep, like a hungry chick, calling to its mother from the nest. Seán pocketed his pipe, walked toward the wreck, and knelt down with a crackle and a groan to see a tiny grey kitten huddled in the shadows in a soft little mound.

"Who are you, then?" Seán reached under the skeletal boat and took the kitten in his hand. It fit in his palm like a little ball of wool with murky, half-seeing eyes. "You're too young to be on your own. Where's your mother and the rest of your litter?" His hand began to vibrate with a loud, rolling purr, almost too large to be coming from such a tiny creature. "Well now, you're lucky it's me who found you and no one else. I'm not one for leaving young ones to die on their own. We'll find you someone to care for you, don't you worry." He put the kitten in his breast pocket, went to buy tea, sugar, bread, and other supplies for his bare pantry, then to collect his mail from the post office. "I've just got one more stop to make," Seán said gently to the sleeping kitten in his pocket as he raised his fist to the priory door.

"How are you, Father?"

"Seán! I'm glad to see you! I'm all right, but how are you?" Father Martin looked Seán up and down with an expression of concern that irked the old man.

"I thought I'd come and see you. I've brought you a bit of cod fresh caught this morning if you'll have it."

"That's kind of you. What do I owe you?"

"Nay Father, it's a gift. It was good of you to come all the way to Thréig for my Muireann's rite of committal and burial. It's a hassle to get there, I know, and you've your responsibilities here, but it meant a great deal to Muireann to be buried on Thréig, and to me as well. It'll be a blessing to me if you let me thank you in this small way. Anyway, being Friday, I imagine you'll be wanting a bit of fish for your supper."

"You're right there. Thank you. Thank you, Seán. And how are you holding up?" he asked again, wise apparently to the fact that Seán hadn't answered him before. "Have you considered my suggestion at all, of moving into town?"

"Oh no, no. I'll just keep on as I am. As I said before, I've no intention of leaving her all alone up there. But Father, I've found something today—I thought you might want it." Seán took the tiny, sleeping kitten from his breast pocket to show the priest.

"A kitten is it!"

"It was crying down on the shore all huddled up under an old currach. Not a brother or a mother in sight. I thought you might take it. Sure, every

priest needs a parish cat, unless they make you sneeze. And this one seems friendly, but far too small to be left on its own. A bit of milk to start out then some soft fish would put some flesh on him."

"I wish I could, but I've already got a cat. Marmalade . . . he's the right color, but nothing like so sweet. He's good enough to me most of the time, but he doesn't take kindly to other cats. He's a bit of a bully, and I fear that little one wouldn't find a safe home with me."

"Ah . . . now that's a shame." Seán said, stroking the sleeping kitten with one finger between its soft, papery ears and thinking.

"Perhaps you could take it back to the island with you. It seems happy enough in your hand there, and it might make you a good mouser when it grows."

"I don't know, Father. I'm old. I haven't any business taking on a young thing that will likely outlive me and wind up homeless again and left to pillaging bird nests. Can you not think of someone in the village who might take him?"

"No, I try to help with the strays when I can, but we've got far too many running around the village to keep up with as it is. We're coming to the end of kitten season now; thanks be to God. I doubt I could find some-one willing to take one so small. It'll be needing a bottle and a lot of care, from the look of it, if it's to survive. Surely it's nowhere near weaned and it looks half perished now. But . . . " Father Martin looked at Seán shrewdly out of the corner of his eye, "all that considered, maybe the kindest thing is to put it in a sack and toss it into the sea, if there's no one willing to care for it. Better than starving to death on the roadside or ravaged by dogs, wouldn't you agree?"

"Nay, Father! Throw him into the sea? You mustn't even think such a thing! I'll take him, if it's between life alone on an island with an old grump and death in the sea! I'll take him. I hadn't wanted a cat, but I'll not see a little one drown or starve!"

"You're a compassionate man. It does you credit."

"Well, I can't abide cruelty and waste, that's all."

"No, nor can I."

"Have you never seen a soul drowning, Father? It's no kindness! It may be quicker, but the terror! The almighty terror! It's no kindness at all!"

"No, it certainly isn't."

"I'll take him, them." Seán knit his brow, sniffed, and put the sleeping kitten back into his breast pocket with his tobacco pouch.

"Thank you, Seán. I'm glad to know he'll be in your kindly hands."

"I must be going if I'm to keep him. He needs feeding," Seán said.

"I thought you might like to sit and talk a while. Have a cup of tea with me. I usually have one at this time."

"Another time, Father. I'd like to be back before the rain comes. I can feel it will be soon. And this wee'un might not make it if I don't get a move on." Seán took his leave of the young priest and taking the kitten with him into his boat, began rowing back to Thréig.

That Father Martin was a bit conniving, Seán decided as he rowed along against the lapping waves. It was clear as anything that he wouldn't have tossed that poor creature into the sea. He just wanted Seán to take him, and he knew it. Surely he could have caught the priest out in his fib—said something like "sure, that *is* the kindest thing at this point," and watched as Father Martin suddenly knew of just the person to take the kitten. Something had stopped him, though.

7

SEÁN CARRIED HIS SACK of supplies up to the cottage and stowed them away. It made him feel suddenly very secure to have a full tea canister and he sighed in relief. He built up the fire and put the kettle on to brew some straight away. His head ached from the strain of going to town and talking with people. It ached from his missed cup of tea that morning, and his weeks of poor sleep. As he sat for a moment waiting for the kettle to boil, a thin frantic voice cried from his pocket, jolting him into action. Needly claws snagged the weave of his shirt as the kitten scrabbled its way up the front of him, wailing, wailing.

Seán leapt to his feet looking around, searching for something he could use as a bottle. The thing was so tiny, it would need to have something to suckle, but what did he have? Seán scowled at the bedroom door, edging toward it reluctantly. His hand wavered over the knob. The kitten's desperate cries grew louder with every passing second. With a deep breath for courage, he knit his brow, turned the knob, and entered the bedroom for the first time since Muireann's death.

He paused in the doorway staring at the empty bed, its blue and white quilt undisturbed this past month. He had thought to never enter it again, that terrible vacant room. To seal it up like a shrine to her memory. The weeping kitten was scrambling and squirming at the side of his pocket. Seán held it still against his chest with his large left hand. Firm handling seemed to calm the kitten and it quietly nestled into him.

Seán's eyes traveled the room from corner to corner. Muireann had seen little beyond those four walls during the years she was bedridden, except for the view from one well-placed window overlooking the sea. There was a time when he wondered whether it was her lack of mobility that kept her in bed or her lack of hope. The one seemed to dwindle in proportion to the other. He ventured in a step more and felt the weight of what he must

find, and what he must do to it. He knew it must be somewhere in the chest of drawers, but he feared digging through all those years' worth of memories that smelled so much of his wife.

What was that scent? He'd never really known what it was that smelled so strongly and singularly of Muireann. She didn't wear perfume or use any different soap from him. It was simply *her* and it only existed here where she had lived and died. A round, soft, comfortable smell. He stepped lightly toward the chest of drawers, avoiding the squeaky floorboard as he had done a thousand times in order not to wake her. He looked it up and down, faltered, and lay down in her place on the bed instead, with the kitten still clutched to his chest.

He looked out the window at that fine blue-gray line where the sky and the sea touched. The rain hadn't started yet, but the sky was heavy with potential. Still, the sea looked so calm—deathly and still—like the quilt without a sleeper beneath it, making it rise and fall with breath. He looked at the ceiling, at the texture of the plaster. She had said she saw angels in it. Angels, fish, faces. . .he never saw anything in the plaster, and didn't see anything now.

Seán stood up, smoothed out the spot where he had lain, and plumped the lonely pillow out of habit. Again, he fixed his gaze on the chest of drawers, this time with determination. He slid open the top drawer. A wave of vertigo washed over him as he gazed down at all the neatly folded stockings, undergarments, and soft embroidered handkerchiefs. Surely he shouldn't disturb them. Surely these little things ought to rest in peace where she had left them. With a deep breath and shaking hand, Seán lifted each item gently, almost reverently as though examining the contents of a reliquary. Where were they?

Finally, at the bottom tucked near the back of the drawer, he found them! A pair of creamy white soft, kidskin gloves. He stared at them. He knew she would have laughed at his hesitation. She would have laughed at his seriousness and urged him on. *Let me have a hand in saving him,* she would have said. He smiled at that. She never could pass up a pun. He picked them up.

Seán had given them to her so many years ago, and she had rarely dared to use them for fear of damaging the gift. She'd said they were too extravagant for someone like her. *Like what?* She had deserved everything he could give her, and he could never have given her everything she truly deserved. Still, she'd kept them perfect, like new, and had worn them only

for special occasions. She had worn them last for Easter Mass before she'd become too ill to leave home. He lifted them almost sheepishly to his nose, breathing in her lingering scent along with the ghost of incense smoke, leeks, and roast spring lamb that still suggested the feast of Feasts. He pressed them to his heart, by the hungry kitten. She would have wanted this. She would have insisted.

With jaw firmly set, but heart knocking about in his chest, Seán picked up the scissors. Just a snip, but it felt like he'd cut her own finger—or his own. Still, it was done, and he tucked its uninjured mate in his left breast pocket, as near to his heart as he could get it.

*   *   *

Seán sat with the kitten in his chair by the fire. "I know it's not what you're used to, but it will have to do. Thanks be to God you're not picky." The tiny kitten latched onto the little finger of Muireann's Easter glove, the one with the hole snipped in the end of it and sucked the warmed milk with zeal. When the kitten had had its fill, Seán took a wet rag and cleaned it. "Aha, a boy-child, I see," he said. "Well, that helps me name you." The kitten climbed up Seán's shirt with needly claws and curled up under his chin.

"You're gray like a dolphin, and when you're grown up, you'll be nearly as sleek, with any luck. I could call you Dolphin, but Finn comes off the tongue easier. Finn will do for you. And with Muireann's wee finger in your mouth didn't you look to be sucking your thumb like Fionn mac Cumhaill, taking into yourself all the wisdom of the world from the salmon of knowledge? We'll see if you live up to the name." The kitten closed his eyes and continued to purr. "Well, Muireann, look at the state of your glove now!" He turned the soggy article over in his hand and smiled weakly. "And you'd have laughed. Even if I hadn't dared do it, you'd have done it yourself without a second thought to nurse the wee babe." Seán laid down the desecrated relic, and paused, examining his own hand in the flickering lamplight.

"Doesn't that hand look just as tough and wrinkled as a smoked fish! That's my father's hand, not mine!" The appalling notion crossed his mind that he was actually turning into his father, and he knotted the calloused fingers into a fist, eying the thing as though he'd never seen it in his life before. He sniffed, released his fingers, and picked up the packet of mail he'd brought with him back from town. He glanced through the few envelopes, hoping as always for a letter from Callum, and feeling, as always,

disappointed to find none. Two letters did arrest his attention, however, and he squinted at words neatly inscribed on the back. They were in his own handwriting.

"But this is . . ." he faltered, hesitated, then tore one of them open. *Come home, son. Come home and say your last goodbyes to your poor mother while you still can*, he'd written weeks ago. Seán tore open the other to find the letter he'd sent the day she had died entreating his son to come to him. *You're all I have left, Callum. Please come.* He had begged—something he had never done in his life before. Seán had his pride, and he blushed to read his own words again, written in such a tone of weakness and despair. He remembered the dark moment he'd written them and was almost relieved that his boy hadn't read them. But these letters had never even been opened at all. Callum had never received them.

It was a sleepless night that followed as Seán sat brooding in his chair, watching the heaving glow of the embers and feeling the rattle of Finn's purr on his shoulder. Why, this changed things. It changed things quite drastically. A pang of guilt stabbed him for the anger he'd felt when Callum didn't show up to the funeral mass or even reply to his letters. Of course their Callum would have come if he had known the state of things. The boy loved his mother dearly. He had always clung to her and saw her as somehow magical. She *was* magical, it was true. She'd had a real gift for storytelling and could make the simplest things seem special just by her way of telling them—the words she chose, the twinkle in her eyes, and of course the singing lilt of her voice. It may be true, Muireann had a tendency toward exaggeration, but no one ever minded that. She was magic . . . she was pure magic.

Seán recalled how Callum used to stare up at his mother, enthralled and engrossed in whatever story she told, leaning his head against her knee. He also recalled the concern he'd felt, himself, when it became evident that the boy preferred his mother's company, sitting by the fire and knitting or listening to her read, rather than coming out in the boat with him or going off with the few boys of his own age left on the island. Yes, that was the start of it—the start of the trouble between himself and his boy.

Seán remembered the dark morning he hauled Callum out of bed and said he wasn't to sit home with his mother anymore. Knitting and reading and baking bread weren't fit occupations for a great big boy of his age. Seán himself had been in harness all his life, and this boy was too soft. It was time

he grew some muscle and some manliness—got some scars and faced the wild and raging sea. It was time he learned his father's trade.

Was he eight then? Nine? Perhaps it wouldn't have hurt him after all, those days spent alone with Muireann. But Seán feared to see his son—his one and only son for whom he had waited and prayed—grow up to be soft and idle. It just wasn't right.

Perhaps he'd overreacted, those years ago. Perhaps it hadn't been fair after all. He recalled the look in the boy's eyes, and how it had angered Seán beyond reason to see the tears streaming down those round cheeks when he slit open the pollock's soft white belly.

"Where did you think your food was coming from, Callum? Did you think your mother was digging the fish out of the garden beds like potatoes? Wipe your eyes, boy, and clean your blade."

Seán leaned his cheek into Finn's soft fur as the kitten slumbered on his shoulder and pressed his hand to the unmarred glove in his breast pocket. *I was too harsh. I shamed him for his gentleness.*

"He's just compassionate, Seán," Muireann had said, when he sat brooding over his pipe, listening to the muffled sobs of the boy hiding in the garden, behind the stone wall, comforted by an old sheepdog. "He has compassion for creatures, like someone else I once knew. Have you forgotten him?"

She was right, of course. She was always right. But even though he understood—even though he knew the boy's compassion was nothing to fear, he heard his own father's words come pouring from his mouth whenever he opened it in his son's direction. Felt them bubbling up like lava and burning his own throat as he spat them out.

Was there no hope at all in this world for fathers and sons? To move past the curse of becoming the very thing you most hate—most fear—of saying the very words that once cut you to the bone as though the wound must somehow be shared for generations to come? Well, perhaps Callum had been right to leave after all, though it had broken his mother's heart. Yes, perhaps he had been right to get off the island while he could and try, in his way, to escape the curse. But where had he gone? Where was Callum now, that he didn't receive his letters or give a new address? Where was he living his life, blissfully ignorant of his mother's passing and his father's sorrow?

8

FROM THE MOMENT CALLUM could climb with confidence, he took to finding little narrow ledges on which to perch on the grey-pink granite sea cliffs. Seán would often see his huddled form against the guano-streaked rock face, motionless and staring, while he himself skirted the headland hauling up nets and lobster creels below.

"What were you looking at up there, son?" Seán would later ask the child. This was before Callum spoke much. Muireann had used to worry about that, Seán recalled. The boy had been so quiet, and had seemingly so few words, she'd feared he was simple—a little soft in the head, perhaps. "What were you looking at way up there on the cliff?"

"Bowds," the boy had said in his high, hushed voice.

"You like the birds, do you?" Seán pursued. Callum had looked up at his father's face with wide, disbelieving eyes.

"No."

"Then why—"

"I wuv'em!" Seán had laughed. In a moment his boy seemed to go from a silent, brooding, and inscrutable egg to fledgling person with interests of his own and a sense of humor. That evening the little boy who had never seemed to have any words, poured forth his questions and little observations about the birds of the cliffs and shores and fields—their habits and names. Not soft in the head after all, Seán had thought at the time. Just quiet, unless the subject matters to him, a little like himself. And the subject for Callum was, and always would be after that: birds.

It was the seabirds that first called to Callum from his hidden perch on the cliff, for they were his island neighbors, ever-present as they lived out their own mysterious destinies before him. The heavy, meaty gannets with their masked faces, the cruel icy blue depths of their eyes, their collective trumpeting bellows. The kind, gentle-looking faces of the kittiwakes that

bely their own fierceness and intrepid nature—their cries of *kittiwaaaaak—kittiwaaaaak* vibrating through the salty air from wide, red, gaping mouths. The speed and violence of the diving guillemot—capelins' scourge—sprats' bane—terror of the high seas. When Muireann gave the boy a little notebook for drawing pictures, he would take it with him to all his rupestral haunts and draw scribbly little forms that he'd said were birds. When Seán mistook a kittiwake for a haystack, Callum was less forthcoming in showing his sketches and hid the little book, along with his collection of stones, shells, bones, and feathers, in a box under his cot.

He watched also the long-billed shorebirds—the curlews, oystercatchers, and spoonbills as they came picking through the shingle for mudworms and little shellfish at low tide. He picked along after them, collecting the empty shells they left behind, and filling his pockets with wet, sandy treasures. When his specimens began to reek with decay, Muireann had insisted that all formerly living treasures spend a few weeks drying out in the sunshine atop the stone wall before coming inside the cottage. How the boy had wept when Seán cleared them away by accident.

Callum met new birds when he started going for his lessons at the little island schoolhouse situated at the other end of the island. To get there, Callum cut through boggy hills along sheep paths, through meadows of bog cotton, and the fields of small neighboring farms, past the lough where glaucous gulls congregated—headless bodies balanced upon spindly pink legs. He would creep past them as near as he could to see their yellow eyes peal open from their slumber, watching him from beneath wind-wimpled feathers—but never so near as to disturb their trust. He especially admired the eiders and divers that lingered near the pier at the little eastern port and the old schoolhouse while he sat eating his lunch.

On one of those walks to school on a cool early April morning, prior to the children being released for the sunny months to labor alongside their parents, Callum encountered an unassuming stranger who would come to determine his future. As the boy strolled through the hilly, windswept fields of nodding bog cotton, budding but not yet in flower, toward the eastern shore and the schoolhouse, Callum heard a piercing, grating voice that sliced through the air and hung on it like a salty mist. Surely he'd heard that voice every summer night and early dawn he could remember, but the sounds of the night and drowsing hours become so much a part of the dreams accompanying them that the sound itself is taken for a dream as well. Callum stopped in his tracks at the ratcheting guttural rasp like a

giant beetle, or perhaps like two notched sticks rubbed together, or a finger running down the teeth of a comb. It seemed to come from nowhere and everywhere all at once: *Crrrrrex!*

Callum stalked quietly toward what he felt must be the source of the sound until a flutter of wings startled him. A brown speckled rail took to low frantic flight before him, rippling the tall stems of bog cotton, shaking their buds in its wake, and disappearing into the dense tangle of grasses fifty feet or so away. He crept toward the spot where he had seen it land, but never could find the bird again.

Callum was tardy arriving to school that day, but Miss Alexander was an understanding schoolmistress with a naturalist's bent herself. She kept him after lessons to hear his description of the strange creaking bird in the field. Since the day he had announced his love for birds, it had been his obsessive mission to know them all by name. His mother had taught him to name the lapwing, cormorant, shag, razorbill, and guillemot even when he barely had words for such simple things as milk and bread. But this secretive bird that hid its identity and called out in the gloaming to find its own kind, was strange and somehow more compelling than all the rest. It was Miss Alexander who finally gave him its name.

When Muireann came looking for her boy, so late had it gotten to be, she would always tell of how he ran to her shouting over and over again the name: *corncrake—corncrake—Corn-Crake!* How that word clipped and croaked like the bird itself. A name, a call that seemed to haunt Callum all that day—all that night, and week, and the summer that followed. He would lay in his bed at night staring into the darkness, his sperm whale tooth clasped to his chest, and whisper into the silence: *Corncrake.*

During the summer breeding months, Callum began to rise in the night to listen to the male's courting call, until he became nearly nocturnal, slipping out between midnight and dawn to creep into the fields and sit, straining his eyes to see their covert movements in the darkness. Seán would notice him slipping back into the garden, even as he prepared to take the boat out before sunrise. Neighbors told him later how the child would sit in their fields, still and quiet as a stone, just listening to the strange calls echoing through the summer air. The little formless scribbles in his notebook started taking on the distinctive suggestion of a corncrake, and the box of treasures under his bed began to collect mottled brown feathers.

Most of Callum's summer days were spent dutifully learning his father's trade, filling the big creels with their wriggling catch, baiting the

lobster creels with the heads and guts, dropping and hauling, dropping and hauling, then rowing their watery harvest over to the mainland to sell. As soon has his duties were fulfilled, the boy would slip off into the mainland hay fields to look for corncrake nests while his father took a drink at the pub. Seán would sip his glass slowly, pensively, hearing only vaguely the tripping melodies coaxed from the traveling fiddler's bow. But he couldn't fully attend to the songs and stories as his mind lingered on his boy's growing obsession and what it all meant.

Soon enough summer fled the island, and with it the corncrakes and all their peeping, weeping children, now precociously mobile. They migrated to the warmer south and stole Callum's heart away with them. He grew sullen in their absence.

"He grieves them like a first love lost!" Muireann had told Seán one day. They could never quite understand what Callum saw in the speckled brown birds, and Callum could not have told them back then. All he knew was that they were part of each other—himself and the corncrakes—and in finding them he had somehow also found himself. Happy was the autumn evening when he brought home the bird book that Miss Alexander had lent him from her own shelf at home. He lingered on that one page tracing the form of the corncrake with his finger and reading over and over about its habits of migration, nesting, and breeding.

"You see, Callum?" Muireann had said, peering over his shoulder at the page, "a book can be a treasure."

9

S UMMERS CAME AND WENT and each one found Callum taller, his voice deeper, his interest in the corncrakes more persistent and urgent even than when he was a little boy running in the fields looking for nests and feathers. He learned that certain returning corncrakes could remember him from season to season and approached him in expectation of his shared pocketfuls of chicken scratch. Seán bristled at the boy's tears when he told of a nest destroyed during the hay harvest—of the female, reluctant to abandon her clutch. Callum had discovered her, a broken heap of disheveled feathers and protruding bone splayed out across the desecrated nest. Beneath her, crushed eggs oozed red and yellow with partially formed chicks and smeared yolk.

"Spare us your tears, Callum! It's just one nest, after all. What's that compared to a good harvest?"

Seán eventually shut his mind to Callum's outbursts, as he did to most things that irritated him, until they became part of the background noise, blending into the constant voiceless wailing of wind and wave. He barely heard them and failed to notice when the wailing stopped altogether. Callum became increasingly private about his passion for the birds. Eventually the boy kept his concerns and interests exclusively between himself and Miss Alexander, who continued supplying him with longer, thicker books about birds until one late spring day he rushed home from school, cheeks glowing with pride and excitement.

"I'm to go over to the mainland to meet a real ecologist! He's giving a talk at the parish hall, and we're to have tea with him, me and Miss Alexander, to talk about birds!"

"What's a man like that doing here of all places?" Seán wondered aloud.

43

"He's come from Dublin to make a survey of the corncrakes nesting throughout the county! I'm to tell him about the colony here that I've been studying!"

"Studying, is it? I didn't know they called staring and drawing pictures studying. Still, you might get a bit of cake out of it."

It was that teatime, that chance meeting, that had proved decisive for Callum's future, though Seán hadn't thought much of it at the time. Muireann dressed the boy in his Sunday best and sent him on his way with instructions not to be greedy about the sweets. Seán considered it all a lot of bother over nothing and went off to smoke his pipe in peace.

The morning after, however, found Callum uncharacteristically sullen as he sat with his father in the currach, bobbing up and down on the waves, hauling up traps.

"What's eating you, Callum? You've scarcely said two words together."

"Nothing." Callum scowled and looked back toward the cliffs and home.

"Are you feeling poorly? Too many sweeties with your tea yesterday?"

"I'm fine," his voice said, though his face disagreed.

"Did you not like going with your teacher and talking about birds?"

"I did."

"And meeting the man from Dublin?" Callum's eyebrows drew together in an even deeper scowl. *That'll be it.* Seán thought to himself. *The big city man made my boy feel small about his drawings and his feathers.*

"Not to your liking then?"

"What?"

"Your big city scientist."

"He was fine."

"Well, what is it then?"

Callum examined his father's face as if to determine whether it would be quite selfish of him to share the burden of a secret so terrible as the one he bore on his shoulders that morning.

"Well . . . it's the corncrakes," he said at last.

"Those wee brown birds you go on about? What's the matter with them?"

"They're disappearing . . . going away."

"Disappearing! *Psh!* I hear them all summer long. Such a racket they make, too, in the middle of the night!"

"That man from Dublin—he's an ecologist, Da. Do you know what he does? His work? He studies the land and its health—"

"Does he now! Sounds like back-breaking labor that!" Seán spat scornfully.

"He came to count the corncrakes still nesting here because they've been disappearing in other parts of Ireland where they used to nest in huge numbers."

"Nonsense! Why would they be disappearing? He's probably just looking in the wrong places at the wrong seasons. They travel around! Everyone knows that!"

"No, Da. He knows where they ought to be and when they ought to be there. And he already knows where they're going. It's *why*."

"And what does he say the reason is? Not enough jobs? Higher wages elsewhere?"

"…farming." Callum mumbled.

"What now?"

"Farming," he said a fraction louder.

"The Lord preserve your innocence, child! Ireland has always been farmed. Long as there have been humans here, we've been tilling the earth, and this land is no different. Farming isn't new. It's as old as Adam. You can't blame something so old as farming for new changes in where some silly birds want to be!"

"He says it's the *way* the land is being farmed now. The big farming machines. A man with a scythe can easily cut around a nest in a field. Machines can't show compassion. And what little scraps of wildland we still have are vanishing along with the creatures that live in them. We're becoming a land without predators . . . we're becoming a—"

"A what?"

". . . a wet desert."

Seán was struck by these words and the image they conjured. He thought of the years of mismanagement under British governance that had stripped the western coast of Ireland of tons of its fish—scouring the sea of its normally healthy populations and making the lives of the traditional farmer-fishermen increasingly difficult. Now Ireland managed its own waters, but it had occurred to him to wonder once or twice—though far more lately—whether all the industrialization and mechanization in the fishing industry might eventually cause the small boat fishermen and subsistence farmers such as himself to go extinct entirely. Those who still clung to

traditional island life grew fewer every year as so many were deserting it for migrant work and better opportunities. New nesting grounds with fewer threats to survival.

Once or twice in his more pessimistic moments Seán had even imagined the waters he'd known all his life becoming a fishless desert—and it was those words of Callum's that had made him pause. A wet desert. Could such a thing be allowed to happen these days? Was it even possible? In spite of everything—decades of experiencing the slow depopulation of his island—increasingly meager catches—Seán still believed that big fishing operations meant jobs for many and food for many more. As long as there were still a few fish left for his family, he didn't mind the flotillas of big belching trawlers too much. And as he thought it through, it all seemed quite the same thing. It must be true of the land, as well.

More productive farms growing diverse crops meant fewer hungry children in Ireland, provided the food actually stayed in Ireland and didn't get shipped off elsewhere for further enrichment of a wealthy foreign minority. Seán imagined shiploads of food leaving Ireland's shores while its people starved, ate grass on the roadsides, or left the land for a different one. He imagined backbreaking labor, roads that led nowhere, and mass graves. He was old enough to have heard the stories from those who had lived them. No, a good harvest was worth far more than a few little brown birds taking their leave, if what the big man said was even to be trusted.

"I wouldn't go believing just anything your educated stranger from Dublin tells you." Seán said at last.

"Why would he make up something like that?"

"I don't know, but city folk have strange ideas sometimes, and they are hardly ever good for those who work the land and harvest the sea. As if we weren't the ones putting food on their tables and keeping them fat and comfortable in their fancy city homes."

"He wasn't fancy at all . . . and I believe him," Callum said, sitting up taller on his seat in the bow of the currach, facing his father.

"Believe what you like. You're old enough to have your own opinions. My opinion is that those who farm big tracts of land are glad of a machine that helps them. But mind this, Callum: corncrakes or no corncrakes makes no difference to us fishermen. As long as there's fish in the sea, we'll eat. I daresay the world will go on turning with one less little brown bird making a racket in its fields at night."

Callum stared silently down at his feet, and Seán took up the oars again to pull them back toward the shore. Their haul was scant, but sometimes it was, after all. Callum sat blankly mulling over his father's words as if some realization was forming and taking shape in his mind like an enormous looming cliff that had hitherto been shrouded in fog.

10

"SAINT MOBHI OF GLASNEVIN was Colmcille's soul's friend. Do you know what that means, Callum? His soul's friend?"

The young man shook his head as he folded himself cross-legged on the floor by the fire. He'd long since stopped sitting at Muireann's feet.

"It means Saint Mobhi was his spiritual father. An elder who advises *like* a father in spiritual matters. And really every matter is a spiritual matter, isn't it? Every soul needs a friend. A friend to whom it can unburden itself when doubts and fears threaten to tear our sails and leave us adrift and far from our charted course. Well, Saint Mobhi was that friend to Saint Columcille's soul.

"It happened that a terrible pestilence had caused Saint Mobhi to send Saint Collumcille, for his own protection, away from Glasnevin back to his own land. There our Saint prayed most fervently that the pestilence would not follow him to Tir-Connell. His prayers were answered, and his kinsmen were preserved from the dread illness.

"Being now ordained a priest of the Church, Saint Collumcille was offered a beautiful parcel of land on the northern coast by his cousin the Prince of Ailech, for all of his kinsmen were eager that Saint Columcille should found a church and a monastery in their lands. But even with such a handsome offer, Saint Columcille refused."

"Refused? Why? Wouldn't that have been a good deed?" Callum asked, half-heartedly shifting the smoldering peat about with the poker.

"It might have been, but even a good deed can be done out of season, and Saint Columcille had no blessing from his spiritual father to be founding churches or monasteries yet."

"But he was ordained. He was a priest—a monk—he saw visions."

"Even very great and holy Saints are under authority, Callum, and he had to await permission from his spiritual father before he undertook a task

of that kind. You remember the pestilence? The terrible affliction that was spreading throughout the land, causing not only sickness but *fear* of sickness and of death? It had already claimed the life of Saint Columcille's dear friend, Saint Ciaran, and it had eventually laid even Saint Mobhi himself on his deathbed. It was at this time that Saint Mobhi finally sent his blessing to Saint Columcille to found a church in the land of his birth. Then, and only then, did our Saint accept the land from his cousin."

"Derry."

"Yes. Daire was surrounded by the Foyle and by marshes so that it was almost like an island, though not so forbidding as Aran, where Saint Columcille had slept on the rocks with Saint Enda and Saint Ciaran years before. Daire was thick with beautiful ancient oak trees back then, and Saint Columcille would not see a single tree cut down to make room for his church and monastery cells. It was a place where God blessed Saint Columcille with many an angelic visitation. Sure, maybe you'll have a vision someday. Maybe you'll see the angels."

Muireann picked up her knitting and fell to softly humming and smiling to herself as Callum sat staring at the glowing embers. This story had always irritated him, but now it filled him with worry, like the very ground under him might sink and swallow him up. He wished he could simply tilt his head to the side and shake this new worry out through his ear like seawater after a swim. It nagged him throughout the day and the following night. Would *he* need permission? Permission to *leave*? Would he need a blessing to do something different with his life? Would it be wrong if he were to decide for himself what his life should be like with or without approval or blessing from home? He had received a vision long ago. He knew he had. He felt its urgency, though there had been no angels in it. Perhaps *because* of that.

But Columcille was a Holy Saint. Great spiritual endeavors were perilous to those who undertook them, and terrible things befell those who were not ready and did not heed their elders. Surely *this* was different. Surely one did not require a blessing to study birds and learn how better to protect them. Wasn't that what man was made for, after all? Placed in a garden to care for the animals, to name them, and know them? And a pretty shoddy job he was doing of it, too, with the corncrakes leaving and all. Something was going terribly wrong, and the corncrakes were only one symptom of many. Surely Callum didn't need permission to do what was right when so

few people realized that there was even anything wrong. He had a duty as one who had received and understood the warning.

Yet Callum lay sleepless in his bed that night. The dawn found him, eyes red-rimmed with lack of sleep, lowering the nets with his father, as he had done in his summer holidays from school since he was eight years old. The boat rolled and pitched in the wake of a passing trawler, and Seán shook his fist at the unheeding captain in annoyance. When the noise of its engine was little more than a rumble in the blue distance, Callum scoured his own depths for courage.

"Da, can I ask you something?"

"What is it?"

"Would you be prepared to give me your blessing if I should choose a life that's different from this? Different from yours, I mean?" His own voice sounded muffled and far off to him, and he feared his father mightn't have heard him, as he had barely heard himself. But he waited all the same.

"How different?" Seán finally asked. He'd had in his mind that the boy would be asking to become a priest or a monk eventually. It was surely his mother's hope and dream for him, though Seán would've liked him to stay and fish with him. He'd become used to the boy's company. Still, in deference to his beloved wife's belief in Callum's high spiritual calling, Seán had determined for many years now that upon such a request, he would embrace his boy and give his heartiest and most eloquent blessing. "How different do you mean?"

"Quite different . . . and far from here," Callum said vaguely, haltingly.

"Spit it out, boy. What is it you want to do?"

Callum took in a deep breath and produced the words he'd practiced, over and over in his head all that sleepless night:

"I feel I will never be satisfied with a life that is not spent in studying birds and doing what I can for their health and welfare, and that of the land that I love. I can do that best by going to university in Dublin and learning everything I can. Miss Alexander has helped me to gain acceptance for the upcoming autumn term. Her brother has kindly offered me a room in his family's home as well as a job at his firm to pay my way. I only ask your blessing before I go."

University? Dublin? And still on about the birds, as though birds were a profession. Seán thought to scold the boy for such wild and foolish dreams, but most of all for keeping secrets from him. He felt his own father's voice clawing at his throat to come out of his mouth in a wild, sarcastic

snarl. With all his strength, Seán struggled against it, but couldn't produce a sound otherwise. He wasn't sure what the right thing was to say anyway. He sat silently, looking down at a broken lobster creel that he pretended to mend, but ended up breaking more badly instead. It seemed to him that this "blessing" his son wanted was little more than an afterthought—a mere formality on his way to doing just as he pleased. He had never even asked Seán's advice about whether it was right for him to leave and do something else so wholly unheard of, or whether there was any secure future in it at all. It seemed to him that the boy's mind had been made up a long time, and that all this song and dance about a blessing was merely that, and he didn't feel like singing along. Seán ground his teeth shut against any words at all, as he knew none he could produce just then would be the right ones.

Callum sighed and looked up at a kittiwake circling low above the boat, white and delicate, its flight feathers gilded in sunlight. Even if it was just scanning their boat for spare fish heads, the corner of his mouth turned upward slightly as he imagined the freedom it must enjoy, riding the air currents with such grace. But his face fell back to sorrow as he thought of the pain he must be causing his father, and he kept silence. The two men merely drifted on somnolent summer waves, deep in their own thoughts, both wishing for something to say.

That evening at supper, the little family table was silent but for the sound of spoons scraping bowls. Muireann reached across the table to squeeze Seán's hand.

"What's the news?" She asked in her low, gentle voice. Seán looked across the table at Callum. The boy had grown to be tall and thin, not really a boy now, but a young man. A young man in shabby trousers too short for him, and a sweater too baggy for him, high shouldered and hunched over his supper, studying the grain of the table like it held the secrets of the universe. Seán drew in a deep breath, summoning every ounce of courage and resolve he could muster. A part of him couldn't help respecting the boy for making up his mind what he wanted and sticking to it. He never could've spoken to his father that honestly, not after the time he had asked him to build a boat with him and go adventuring. Not after the sting of being told his dreams were foolish. How quickly we settle for less in this life, giving up before we even begin . . . and how far Callum must have reached inside of himself to call up that voice and to say what he'd said on the boat.

No, Seán might not approve. He might not even understand. But he was not his father, and he would not prevent his son from leaving home

and finding his own way. Still, he could not find it in himself to offer the blessing Callum wanted. A mixture of fear, anger, and even a jealousy that he couldn't explain coated the inside of his mouth as he cleared his throat to speak.

"Callum's off to Dublin soon, Muireann. You'll want to make sure he has some clothes that fit him properly so his new city friends can't tell he's island-born. Our Callum's going to be a hero, Muireann. A savior to the birds . . . Saint Bird-Shite, himself." He stared down at his son, feeling his words to be out of his control and tumbling out against his own will. He felt himself scrambling to stop them, but he heard himself say in a voice that he despised, "You're a damned fool, Callum. May it bring you nothing but sorrow! But go! By all means, I'll not be the one to stand in your way." With that, Seán rose from the table and took himself down the rocky cliff to the little stretch of sand he liked best. There he sat miserably, trying to gather his conflicting feelings into a clear shape, or at least find some place to put them out of his way for now.

No, he hadn't denied his son the future he wanted, but he'd withheld those words of blessing, the absence of which creates a painful and questioning void in a man's heart. Every day following that one, Seán wished he'd embraced his son and sent him into his strange future with words of kindness and of love. And every day since Old Maeve's untimely death those months past, Seán feared his words that day had stuck to his boy.

11

C ALLUM SAT FOLDED NEATLY in his coach seat, large, gentle hands gripping each other on the sharp creased knees of his new trousers. A shiny new waterproof lay draped in the crook of his long arm, and a raging autumn gale rocked the coach to and fro as it dodged deep ponds in the road. Nervous hands gripped their seats all around him as rain slithered down the windows like tears from above, obscuring the desolate landscape that passed.

Callum half-thought that if the driver were to kick him off the coach and out into the torrent, the weather would miraculously clear up. Surely this was the wrath of God—the consequence of an un-blessed voyage which the elements themselves sought to keep him from making. He thought of his father and the old fishing boat. They would not be out on the sea in such weather. No, his father would have seen this storm coming long before it arrived. He would be in his chair with his pipe, staring at the fire. His mother would be singing snatches of old songs about monks, monsters, manuscripts, and mermaids. He rubbed his swollen eyes and considered the birds.

Yes, the birds . . .

As long as he thought of the birds, he was safe from such misgivings. Only a love like this could tear him from home. Fishing was not bad. Farming was not bad. And his parents were certainly not bad. He would have stayed, even with the island depopulating and subsistence farming becoming less and less tenable an option for survival in these modern times. He would have stayed because he loved them. But this was bigger. This was urgent.

Everything he loved about that island farm—his island childhood— could wash away with the unhealthy tide of overfished waters. Could disappear with the long-lost predators who had kept balance. With the long-lost

forests that had held the good soil, and the dwindling corncrakes that filled the air with their creaking, insect-like song. He had to leave because he loved his island and every living thing on it. He had to leave it in order to save it. It was his heroic mission.

But no one tells you the real cost of being a hero in this world. His mother's stories talked of lofty sacrifice, of courage and bravery and nobility of mind and soul. Of giving up one's life for another in a blaze of glory. Of resurrection and boons from the gods shared with all by the returning hero. The old tales were silent about the almighty embarrassment of it all.

It is easy to step out courageously against a menace of substance that everyone can see and agrees to be a monster. But when you are the only one to see the threat, it is with burning cheeks and hunched shoulders that one must trot like a mouse out to face it amid the jeering laughter and grievous disappointment of those who think you foolish or had dreamed of a different future for you. Those who have received the warnings with apathy or resignation. Those who have shut their minds to it entirely. It takes a thick skin to act heroically. A thick skin impervious to the embarrassment of looking a fool before others.

12

"WHEN I WAS A boy, I had such dreams. I wanted to be an explorer, like Saint Brendan the Voyager. I always wished I'd been named Brendan rather than Seán. Seán was my father's name, did you know that, Finn? And his father's name before him. What a world this would be if men named themselves, after they'd gotten to know themselves a bit. So much of a parent's hopes and dreams go into the naming of a child who more often than not feels trapped by the name he's given. Yes, I could have been a Brendan. Maybe that would have made all the difference.

"When I was a wee'un, I wanted to take a crew of daring men and sail the seas looking to find strange lands no mortal eye had seen. Do you know, Finn," Seán said to the kitten as it purred on his shoulder, "Saint Brendan and his men discovered a new island in the middle of the cold North Sea. They weighed anchor and went ashore to take a look around. It was a fine place to stop for a rest from the waves, and they had just started to make camp with a fire and all when they discovered the island itself was moving. A moving island! Can you imagine! Ha! It was a whale, you see, and there they stood on its back! Well, who's to say if it's true or not. Who's to say what Saint Brendan really saw if he lived at all. Surely he found new islands, even if he didn't make it all the way to North America as they say. And from his great skin currach he'd surely have seen whales humping in those icy waters, but that's how my mother told it—and she could spin a tale, too. Perhaps island life makes storytellers of us all in time."

He reached for his pipe. The movement woke Finn who dug his claws into Seán's shoulder to keep steady.

"Easy now, Finn. This whale's not going under and drown you. I'm just getting my pipe—there we are. You're a grand little fellow to talk to, you know."

Seán ran his finger pensively around the bowl of his pipe, then stuffed it with tobacco, tamping it down with the wide, flat head of an old nail that he kept in his pocket for that purpose. He sucked deep and slow as he held a match just above the dried strands of aromatic leaf until they glowed and smoldered.

"I remember one time I was out fishing with my father. I couldn't have been much more than eight or nine," Seán said, leaking smoke through yellowed teeth. "'Father,' I says to him, 'Father, I've decided I'm going to be an explorer like Saint Brendan. I'm going to build a skin currach large enough to take a sail and a small crew of exceptionally brave men, and I'm going to discover new lands.'" He paused, stroking Finn between his large batwing ears.

"A great boat builder was my father, though that wasn't what put bread on the table. Jack of all trades, you might say, as a man must be out here. Built at least five fine currachs in his life that I can remember. Likely others that I don't. Built the cottage for my mother. He built the beds we slept on and the chairs we sat on. We still eat on the table he built. Good with wood. Good with his hands. A good man all 'round, I think, now that I'm old.

"'Will you help me, Father?' I says to him. 'Will you help me to build this great big boat, and will you join my expedition? We could go together, just you and me and maybe Patch—that was our old sheep dog . . . poor old Patch! We could go together, just you, me and Patch and we could discover new lands!'" Seán scratched the kitten's head as its eyes narrowed to contented slits. "I'll never forget what he said to me that day, nor the look on his face as he said it. He said, 'What fool stories has your mother been telling you? You're getting too big for dreams like that. We're fishermen. Long as there are fish in the sea, we eat, and dress, and keep our wives' heads up in the village. We build currachs for fishing, not for fun.'

"He was quiet for a time, and I stared down at my feet. I remember because I thought if I didn't look at him, he mightn't look at me. I didn't want him to look at me . . . but he did. 'Your reading, writing and numbers are good enough to be done with school,' he told me. 'You'll come out with me from now on and make yourself useful in the boat.' And that was that. I've fished ever since. And Patch, my first mate in make believe, didn't much outlive my dream. Father shot him when it turned out he was worrying sheep. It wasn't out of cruelty or even revenge. I know that now, though it was hard to believe back then. Sheep worrying is a capital offense for a retired sheepdog, especially when your very survival and your neighbor's

depends on just a few beasts. Anyway, that was about the end of my boy-hood dreams. I don't blame him, really, I don't, and it's not been all bad. It's a good life I've had here on this cliff with Muireann, and with Callum before he left. A good life. Though I never thought I'd be the father to shame my own son for wanting something different."

Seán watched out of the corner of his eye as the embers of his pipe glowed orange with each puff, like the fiery creature whose warm belly rested in his hand was breathing softly in sync with him. Chill was that late October evening as a sudden wind finally rose up and blasted cold rain against the cottage. The waves below turned dark and capped with foam, even as a crash of thunder shook the cottage, rattling the kettle on the stove and cups in the cabinet. Finn stirred and nestled closer into Seán's neck.

"I could do it, you know . . . I could build that boat and make that voyage. I could see other islands, maybe not new ones, but they'd *all* be new to me. Muireann said it herself, didn't she? *Old men ought to be explorers.* It could be an answer to all of this. If I could just find Callum . . ." And as Seán continued to consider, the prospect seemed to be not only *an* answer, but *the* answer. The *only* answer.

Seán's mind filled and expanded nearly to bursting with the over-whelming desire to live on a boat. To live on a nice big boat and to sail away from everything that he had ever known, everything he had felt duty-bound to preserve, every memory held within that cottage that squeezed his chest with grief, to sail away and explore with his boy.

"I would take him with me if he'd come. He could watch the odd spe-cial birds on the islands that we'd find. I'd let him watch them as long as he liked, drawing pictures and collecting feathers as he did when he was small. We'd fish still, but just for us. I would clean them. I don't mind it anymore. He never liked that bit, but I would do it."

The kitten stretched and yawned, its rough, pink tongue curling back like an ocean wave, tucked its legs up under itself and rested in a soft, round heap. Seán fell silent and stared long at the peat embers, with the rain drill-ing against his window, the air heavy with pipe smoke and dreams, old and new.

PART II

The Fisherman, the Priest, and the Cat

1

"ISLANDS ARE MYSTICAL PLACES, Callum. Holy men and women have always been drawn to them. Places of quiet solitude where one might encounter God. It is in our blood and our most ancient history, even before Christianity took root in Ireland, to be ever searching for the divine in solitude, yet always, in the end, drawn back into communion with each other.

"It wasn't just our Saint Columcille who loved islands for monasteries. Many people, Christian and Pagan, throughout history have lived out their years on barren shores with boulders for pillows and only the birds and the angels for company.

"There is a beautiful island of the Inner Hebrides called Lismore. Saint Columcille and Saint Moluag both wanted it for a monastery, but neither man would yield to the other, so they agreed on a race to settle their dispute. They both took to their currachs and pulled hard toward Lismore. The first man to touch the island would have the honor of founding a monastery there.

"Well, our Saint Columcille was a strong, vigorous, chiefly man, and he was clearly winning the race. He was just closing in on the shore when Saint Moluag chopped off his own little finger and threw it as hard as he could. His little finger landed on the stony beach, making him the first to touch the island, though his little finger arrived well ahead of the rest of him. So it was Saint Moluag who would build the monastery at Lismore."

"But that's not fair, Mammy! Saint Moluag cheated!"

"He certainly was desperate to have Lismore for his own monastery, wasn't he? Who's to say if it's true, Callum, but as the story goes, our Saint Columcille didn't much like the outcome either. His famous foul temper flared up and he cursed Lismore! He said he hoped poor nine-fingered Saint Moluag would be most unhappy there. Now that wasn't so very charitable either, was it?"

"They were both acting ugly!"

"You'll find as you grow up that life is often this way. Sometimes you'll want something that's good and honorable, and you want it badly enough to take it the wrong way. Show me a man in this world who regrets nothing."

"But they were Saints! The Saints are meant to be holy!"

"And how do you suppose they became holy, Callum? The men and women who gave their lives to the harshness of monasticism did so because they regretted the way they'd lived before, not because they were already holy and wanted to escape from all of us who weren't. They were people just like you, and sometimes very rough men, too, with blood on their hands and past sins to mourn. We all make mistakes. We say things we oughtn't say, or neglect to say the things we should. We soil our conscience and weep and mourn because we're human. But then, we get up, make our peace with God and neighbor, and move on the wiser. Attend to me closely when I tell you that those good people in your life who you think can do no wrong are bound to disappoint you—even deeply wound you. You'll have your chance, like Saint Columcille, to either curse them or forgive them."

* * *

It was unusual for Seán to make more than one trip to the mainland in the space of a fortnight, especially without any fish or lobsters to sell, but the very next morning found him trudging down the cliff with a satchel slung over his shoulder, containing a tiny gray kitten, a little jar of milk, and his wife's old Easter glove. He hadn't slept at all that night; his mind was so busy with thoughts of voyaging and boats. After his tea and double portion of porridge, he decided that he must act quickly before he lost his resolve and returned to that awful waiting. He rowed swiftly across to shore as though the current were urging him on toward his destiny and marched with great purpose down toward the priory.

"Back again, Seán? I didn't expect to see you again so soon. Come for that cup of tea, have you?" Father Martin was in his kitchen garden with shiny rubber galoshes and sleeve garters clipping the thick, stubbled stems of bulging autumn squashes and courgettes and placing them in a large basket.

"Thank you, Father. Yes, I'll be having that cup of tea. I've had something on my mind, and I thought you might be able to help me." An

immense smile spread over Father Martin's pink face at the invitation to help someone, anyone, and he sprang to his feet dusting the soil from his cassock.

"Well, come in, come in. We'll see if Mrs. Kelly might toast us up some potato cakes as well!"

"Oh, don't put her to any trouble on my account."

"It's no trouble! What's a cup of tea without something buttery to go with it?"

"Is your, eh . . . *Marmalade* about?"

"Yes, I believe there's a jar of marmalade. Are you fond of it?"

"No, no . . . you said you had a fierce tomcat."

"Oh, him? He's on his rounds roaming the town this morning—oh, I see!" he said, as Seán lifted the flap of his satchel to show the little gray lump huddled inside. "No, the kitten's quite safe."

Father Martin left his galoshes by the coat rack and led Seán to a seat in his study. Seán sat fidgeting in the fine green velvet-covered chair while Father Martin went to ask his housekeeper for the tea and potato cakes. He looked around the spotlessly clean and tidy office, its bookshelf, rich looking rug with combed-out tassels, and prominent statuette of the Virgin Mother draped in pale blue. She seemed to watch Seán with an amused expression from her little grotto as he took the now weeping kitten from his satchel and let it totter about the room until it begged loudly to be fed. He prepared the jar of milk and the Easter glove.

"Now, isn't that clever! I knew you were just the person to care for that wee'un there. I'm sure I'd never have thought to feed it that way," Father Martin said as he strode back into the study.

"It works well enough for now, until he's gained a bit more strength and flesh," Seán said, stiffening a little and clearing his throat.

"Well now, Mrs. Kelly will have the tea out for us in a minute or so. Why don't you tell me what's been on your mind, my son." Father Martin sat in his leather chair, hands meekly folded on the desk in front of him, and head tilted to one side with a look of kindly patience so terrible that Seán had to look at the priest's nose rather than his eyes.

"Oh, it was just a memory, Father. Part of one at least. I heard some months back that you were planning to make a parish library."

"Yes, indeed. And yes, I did—well, that is to say, it's still growing, but it's in existence."

"Grand, grand . . . and how many books have you?"

"Well, I can't say I've counted them, but a growing number. I shall soon have to catalog them somehow to keep track of them all. I've made a little reading room in the parish hall and the shelves just keep filling up with donations from here and there. I'm always finding new volumes to add when I make my little trips down to Cork. My mother has given me a great load of books from her collection, and from her generous friends."

"Oh . . . that's very nice, very nice indeed . . ." Seán nodded nervously, his head bobbing up and down like a little boat in the wake of a passing trawler.

"Was there a specific book you wanted to see, Seán?"

"Ah . . . well, maybe. I was wondering . . . er . . ."

"Yes?"

"I just thought you might . . ."

"Yes, what is it, Seán?"

"Well, I thought I'd ask if you have any such thing as an . . . atlas."

"Oh, naturally!" Father Martin said, beaming his straight, white smile. "I've a fine large world atlas. Newish, too, I believe. Or at least it's in very good condition if it's not. I'll show it to you after our tea if you like."

"Fine, fine. I'd like that . . . yes."

Mrs. Kelly, a formidable middle-aged widow with sharp features that coincided with her sharp and practical nature, set a tea tray down on a low polished table between the two men. She poured out two steaming cups, evaluating Seán a little suspiciously from the corner of her eye before noticing the furry gray lump making a wet spot on the expensive-looking rug with the combed-out tassels. She scowled and tromped off muttering under her breath.

"Thank you, Mrs. Kelly," Father Martin called obliviously after her. "Lovely, that is!" he said, after sampling the potato cake. He dribbled butter on the lap of his cassock and rubbed ineffectually at it with his handkerchief. "Well, that's unfortunate . . . was there, eh . . . anything else you wanted to ask me, Seán?"

"Well, yes, now you mention it . . . but I doubt you'd have anything like it."

"I might," he said, still rubbing.

"It's not really the kind of thing you'd have in a parish library." Seán looked sheepishly at Father Martin over his cup of tea.

"I'm not sure what you mean," Father Martin said, finally giving up on the greasy stain, which he had enlarged by rubbing it around. "All

knowledge—all truth—is God's business and of interest to me. It's not just heady theology books and old sermons I have. I've got a growing shelf of books on animal husbandry, botany, beekeeping, the brewing of ales . . . and of course there's poetry and the great heroic epics of several ancient civilizations. It's a veritable scriptorium! Or it is now that there's a writing table in it. Tell me, Seán, what is it you're wanting?"

"Well, would you happen to have any books about boats and sailing and navigating and the like?" Father Martin's face beamed again, that bright white boyish grin, and he nearly sloshed tea onto his lap as well as butter.

"How wonderfully providential. You mind how I said most of the books came from my mother's collection, and from her friends?"

"Oh, I see. Of course, you'll have nothing of that sort. Just love stories set at sea."

"But of course I do! Seán, my father was a proud member of the Irish Coast Guard and keenly interested in all things nautical. After his passing, my mother made a present to me of all *his* books for my library. I said it was her collection, but mostly the books belonged to him. I suppose she's still enjoying her nautical romances . . . I jest. She's a very practical woman, but that's neither here nor there. I may only have a few volumes of sermons and theology after all, but if there's one topic well-represented it's boats: boat building, navigation, ocean voyages, lives of great explorers, naval histories . . ."

"Well now, I suppose it is providential then, as you say."

"Apparently so, though you've got me curious now, Seán." Father Martin took another bite of his dribbly potato cake looking the old man up and down through narrowed eyes. "What exactly are you up to?"

2

WHEN THEY'D FINISHED THEIR tea, Father Martin led Seán into the cramped, dark room in the parish hall which he had dedicated to books and catechetical materials for the edification of his flock. It was not so much a small room as a large broom cupboard. "No Archbishop Marsh's Library," as Father Martin put it. No valuable volumes, sliding ladders, nor shelves high enough to necessitate them, but the shelves he had were packed full of everyday wonders and the air was heavy with the quiet, mildewy scent of books.

Father Martin had installed a small reading table with a lamp where his parishioners might sit, if they wished, and leaf through some of the volumes he had acquired, though precious few had taken him up on it before Seán. Father Martin was seized with that righteous pride in the role Irish monastics had played in preserving the literature of classical civilization after the fall of Rome. To him, this little reading room held the significance of an ancient scriptorium, and he held the secret hope that his little library would contribute to saving civilization in its own small way.

"Here's the atlas I was mentioning, Seán. You see what a fine large volume it is. From my father's collection. There's most likely been a bit of geographical renaming and shuffling of powers since—aha! See here! They have us as the *Irish Free State*. So published sometime between 1922 and 1937—looks newer than it is after all. I doubt it's seen much use."

Seán felt that the young priest was showing off and paid his little history recitation only a grunt of acknowledgment. All his life there had been conflicts and treaties, news and rumors of all this shuffling about. Violence and struggle. Collusion and collision. Rarely had Seán felt its reality tucked away as he was on his island. He longed for a unified, home-ruled Ireland without partitions and partisan violence as much as anyone but making

that happen was someone else's problem. There was only one problem in the world that he owned just then.

Seán scratched his chin stubble and examined the jagged coastline laid out before him, searching for his island. Was it too small to even have been put down? It didn't matter. Names might change, politics and powers might roll in and out with the tide, but the land and sea surely couldn't change much in a mere human lifetime, and he knew that little stretch of cliff like the face that greeted him in the washroom mirror every day. He could have drawn in that little sprinkling of islands himself if he'd had to.

"Here's us, Seán." Father Martin pointed to a tiny dot on the northwestern coast denoting a settlement. Seán rested his finger on that spot. His eyes traveled from there around the northern coast, up through the little narrow stretch of ocean to another cluster of islands. It could be done. Of course it could! Saint Columcille had done it in a little skin currach. Perhaps smaller even than what he had planned, for he had only gone as far as the Hebridean Islands. What Seán wasn't sure of was where exactly the saint had launched from. Derry? Or *London*derry as some called it? Muireann would have known, but surely it didn't make much difference. He just wanted to see in general what route he might take for such a pilgrimage as he was scheming.

"If you don't mind my asking, Seán, what is it you're planning?"

"Just a wee trip. It's long overdue, you might say."

"A trip to where?"

"Here." Seán pointed vaguely at the cluster of islands skirting Scotland's southwestern coast. "Iona first and foremost. That's where we'll start. We'll see Saint Columcille's island, for it was Muireann's wish. Then . . . well . . ."

"Then what?"

"We'll make a...well, we'll just have to see." Seán hesitated as he sensed the growing incredulity in the young priest's expression, though he was clearly trying to be encouraging—annoyingly so. Encouraging as only someone convinced of his own superiority might be.

"Make a . . . what, my son?"

Seán hesitated. He couldn't risk the priest thinking his mind had gone strange or senile in his grief. He might try to stop him.

"Oh, we'll see. It's not all planned yet, you know. I'm just starting."

"I see. A pilgrimage, is it? Wouldn't that be a thing! And who's making this journey with you? You said 'we' didn't you?"

"Callum, my son, and me. I need to take him with me, you see. We need to go, and soon. As soon as ever we can. I'm getting no younger, you know."

"You've heard from him, then?"

"No, not yet."

"Then you're making plans for the two of you that he doesn't know about? How do you know he'll be able or even willing to go with you? You said yourself he's a busy man now."

"He *will* come."

"But didn't you tell me only a few weeks ago that the two of you haven't spoken in several *years*? This seems an awfully elaborate gesture, doesn't it? I'd hate for you to be disappointed." Father Martin's eyes had that soft, kindly look to them that they got when he was trying to sound wise and pastoral. But this young priest was treating him like a child who was asking for the moon when *he* was just a child himself! Well, lucky for him, Seán was fond of children and believed himself to be quite gentle with them. He smiled indulgently.

"Have a little faith, Father. It's *you* who should be telling *me* that, not the other way round. Listen, for such a pilgrimage as this will be, I wouldn't be surprised if Saint Columcille himself were to bring my Callum home to me on the wings of a dove. It's a Holy purpose. Holy and good. He'll come. I know he will. I'll keep writing letters and try to locate him through his college, as that's the strongest link I have to his whereabouts. I've not run out of tricks to find him yet. I'll go myself to Dublin and search him out if I must, though I've never set foot there before, and don't relish the thought. When he knows what it is I'm planning, I know he'll come."

Something was shifting and swelling in Seán, and he felt it deep in his chest. It surprised him at first, after those interminable days of darkness and paralysis. It was as though a window had opened in a stuffy room. A window had opened and brought with it the song of the waves slapping and sucking at the sides of a sailing currach, the grating cries of the sea birds, and the laughter of his son by his side. He heard the laughter like that of a child, for he still thought of his son that way. It had to be. The curse was about to be broken and both of them set free. It was hope that swelled in his chest. Hope and anticipation. How pleased Muireann would be if she were looking down upon him now.

Seán's face glowed in a way Father Martin had never seen before. The young priest had only known Seán the caretaker. Seán the devoted nurse.

Seán the fierce and hot-tempered protector, independent and aloof. And most recently, Seán the wounded, grieving, and silent. He hadn't known Seán before all his sorrows, when a smile was not so rare a thing. Now, but for the crags and fissures that carved his face, Seán was like a child. Father Martin wanted to be glad for him. A corner turned in his grieving. A re-discovery of joy and purpose. But surely it was too soon and too much. He couldn't help worrying, for he lived under a curse of his own. He wouldn't dare hinder Seán just then, but he hesitated to be swept along in this strong current of optimism and ambition, lest it prove to be a whirlpool that would swallow them both.

"Well, that sounds very exciting for you. I'd like to help. You come and visit the library as much as you like and study the maps and such. I'll keep a look out for books that might help you. And do keep writing letters. You'll need to reach your Callum as soon as possible. The man needs to know that his mother has died."

3

EEKS PASSED WHERE HARDLY a day wouldn't find Seán rowing over to the mainland with his skinny little gray kitten tucked away in his satchel, bringing a few fish to sell, though far fewer, most thought, than one might expect, to the point that it all seemed a bit perfunctory. People began to wonder at seeing so much of him around the village but decided it must have been loneliness that drove him there. Loneliness and guilt, most likely. Guilt for the godless way he'd gone wielding words of power, and guilt for not taking help when it was offered in kindness. Perhaps he'd received some penance that brought him daily to the parish hall. Some strange, progressive penance that new priests gave out instead of a set number of prayers. Perhaps he was atoning for his sins by alphabetizing Father Martin's books. There was no telling with these young priests.

But the loneliness must have been part of it as well. Life without Muireann must be dreadfully hard to bear, especially with no one else around to talk to. But for the odd seasonal landless fisherman, Seán was now the last of his kind. The last of those tough, intrepid island men to stay on Thréig throughout the harshest seasons, refusing the allure of mainland towns and the promise of a steady wage from industrial fishing operations with their big boats and machines. When the schoolhouse closed, the last of the families with children finally abandoned the island. A child's laughter hadn't been heard on that desolate island for years now.

Perhaps that was why he spent so much time at the priory. Perhaps it was more than a strange penance. Father Martin was close in age to Seán's own child. Perhaps that was what drew him to the young priest who, to be sure, no one else really cared to visit if it could be avoided. He was just so terribly *youthful*. How can one even speak seriously to someone so young? They know nothing at that age, though there's no telling *them* that. And of

course, his position made it so that he had to pretend to know many things that he didn't, and that made everyone uncomfortable.

Yet there went Seán, nearly every day now, knocking on the priory door with some fish or lobster in hand for the young priest. And he would stay far longer than necessary for confirming the state of the weather, trading pleasantries, or having a cup of tea. The village gossips kept track down to the minute of how long Seán stayed with Father Martin, and sometimes it was hours. Had the old man taken up an interest in heavenly matters since the passing of his wife? What else could the two of them find to talk about?

Seán remained blissfully unaware that his presence in the village was causing a stir of speculation amongst those with nothing better to do with themselves than to spy—those who dared not speak to him personally since he'd been so vilely rude to them and their offered kindnesses. Those who still feared provoking his curse. He didn't notice the eyes peering at him from behind curtain lace or over garden walls or hedges. He didn't notice because each of those days brought him some piece of information he hadn't possessed before. Each day brought him closer to a voyage of discovery, a voyage of reconciliation. His Holy calling! And each day made the whole scheme seem less hypothetical and like it could and *would* really happen.

Each day Seán wrote letters querying the colleges, research institutes, the intellectual centers, and clubs in Dublin for any information regarding his son. Each day, he would show up at the post office looking for a response. And each day, it seemed, brought either nothing at all or some brief communication from someone's secretary or other saying that Callum was no longer receiving messages there, and hadn't been for some time. He was simply nowhere to be found, at least in the places where it made sense for him to be. It was time to become a little more creative. Museums, maybe. Cathedrals of knowledge that might keep a bird expert to dust their stuffed specimens and tell dull facts to visiting school children. He'd try that next.

"Wouldn't it be easier to get answers over the telephone, Seán?"

"It might. But I don't like using it. I'd rather write."

"Well, would you like me to make some calls for you?"

"No, no. I don't need that. If I wanted calls made, I would make them myself, but I'd just as soon write. I can say everything I need to say without stuttering and taking up folks' time. I can wait for a letter."

"It would just be so much quicker and easier to make a few calls."

"For you, maybe. I've said I don't care for it."

The truth was that Seán didn't have a telephone of his own, and indeed had only used one a few times in his life. Thréig had no electricity nor running water for that matter (unless one classified the freshwater springs on the island as "running")—things the young priest took for granted. That austere, traditional way of life was increasingly rare and Seán was, to Father Martin, like a living specter of the past: a fascinating specimen. A species in decline.

Those few times Seán had used a telephone had caused him such a case of the nerves that he could barely stammer out what it was he wanted. He felt much more confident that he could get his message across in writing, and he was proud of his penmanship. He'd been leaps and bounds ahead of all the other children in school when he was taken out to fish with his father. He had practiced his joined-up writing with curls and flourishes so that someday when he was an explorer and his ship's log was on display at Trinity College, people would be able to read it and marvel at the things he'd discovered. Well, that was long ago, but the pride in his literacy and fine handwriting remained, and he wouldn't be convinced to make a phone call, easy though it may have seemed to the young priest.

So Seán continued writing his letters, posting them far and wide. He continued reading books. He kept a journal of notes on navigation, seafaring, and the natural history of the Hebrides that he knew would be important later. He carefully traced the page in Father Martin's atlas that showed the Northern coastline of Ireland and the Scottish Isles beyond. He penciled in the route that would take him from his very own cove, skirting along the coast past Arranmore, the Fanad Head lighthouse, and way up to Malin Head. From there the little stretch of open ocean—past Islay, Oronsay, Colonsay—all the way to St Columba's Bay on Iona, as they called it in the Atlas.

It wasn't the open ocean but the jagged coastline, strewn with hidden dangers and unseen rocks and rip tides that worried him. The unpredictable character of the sea and the weather. And there were so many little islands, he could easily end up on the wrong one if he was but a hair's breadth off course. But he assured himself that his journey was blessed. He knew he would make it to Iona and the shore where Saint Columcille landed in his own currach. He must simply find his boy, build his boat, and set sail. The blessing of Saint Columcille himself, and Muireann smiling down on him, would guide his vessel.

4

I T HADN'T BEEN THE easiest of transitions for Father Martin, coming up as he had from the city of Cork with his peculiarly high-pitched regional accent. He arrived all shining and new, still smelling of holy oil and the fresh sweetness of youth and all its attendant naïveté. The superannuated parish priest he was sent to replace had been both local and beloved for the past half century of his tenure. Now, here came Father Martin with his smart haircut, straight white smile, and smooth, symmetrical pink face making changes that no one liked.

Yes, poor Father Martin was much talked of, not really maliciously, but with that condescension which the young particularly despise, as if to say, *this mere babe looks scarcely old enough to light a candle unsupervised.* But it was generally agreed that a few winters and tactful words and nudges might ripen him into a form to their liking, or at least make him tolerable.

One of the chief complaints against Father Martin was his rudimentary grasp of the Irish tongue. That is to say, he spoke it badly but with a terrible confidence that made his parishioners cringe. Oblivious to their discomfort, he would continue on while his listeners fell to examining their shoes in embarrassment for him. His unfortunate linguistic shortcomings had resulted in the majority of Father Martin's parishioners speaking *to* him in English and *of* him in Irish. But one could not fault Father Martin for failing to try. He tried and tried again.

He tried to establish societies for the communal reading of edifying books. He tried to interest the parish in his little library, which he saw in his mind as being his great gift to the community. He tried to establish a little community garden where neighbors might join together in honest toil and share in the fruits of their labors. Such an endeavor was better suited to an urban parish where members were not already busy tending their own gardens, and in many cases, small farms. And they already helped each other

bring in harvests anyway, so Father Martin ended up tending the garden by himself. Cheerfully. Always cheerfully. And of course, he tried to be a shining example of charity and hospitality in the community as any good priest ought. He did this by hosting soup suppers with psalmic recitations during Lent, a tradition of the early monastic communities that he was eager to re-popularize. These events, however, were only sparsely attended by those widowers chiefly interested in a free helping of Mrs. Kelly's good Lenten soup and soda bread, who slithered to the exit before the readings were finished.

All the subtle and less than subtle snubs, the gentle and less than gentle hints from the community, could not dampen Father Martin's enthusiasm and resolve. He continued annoying them all with his youth, his blinding smile, his poor Irish, and his big ideas until he became something of a fixture—put up with, but mostly ignored.

It was only when quiet old Seán, who for the past few years only ever came to the village to sell his catch and barely spoke to anyone anymore, began appearing at the priory door most days that the collective eyes of the village became fixed again on the young priest in baffled interest. Whispers and tutts and speculations continued to run rampant over garden hedges and in the pub all that late autumn, but no one could have guessed the real goings on between the unlikely pair.

One steely late-November afternoon in Father Martin's study, Seán lifted the flap of his satchel and turned out the now plump gray kitten like a pudding onto the rug. His eyes had sharpened into a clear bright yellow and his belly was round and comfortable looking. The sharp bones along his back had receded into a sleek, healthy arch and he'd developed full control over his bladder, as well as the claws in his immense velvety paws. Since graduating from the Easter glove to eating soft fish from a bowl, he had grown rapidly with the promise of developing into an enormous and powerful tomcat. Finn happily went to work swatting at dust motes and lurking beneath the chairs in Father Martin's study while Seán spread open his notebook on the desk with a proud flourish.

"This is the boat I'm going to build, Father. Like the old currachs my father built, but bigger and more stable for the open sea. It'll have a mast, see?" He pushed the notebook across Father Martin's desk. The page showed a swooping, fanciful drawing of a sailing boat cresting a dramatic, curly wave.

"That's a bit of an antique design, isn't it? An open currach and a square sail? These shores are rough and perilous even in something more . . . shall we say modern?"

"It was good enough for Saint Columcille, and Saint Brenden too, I might add. It's what I know how to build. I watched my father. I helped him with his last one and built two others of my own since. I don't want to go getting fancy and experimental when good old traditional Celtic ingenuity will get me there."

"It *might* get you there. The southwest winds beat against this coast in all seasons, as you well know. Who's to say you could even tack out to sea, against the wind, without being swept back to shore and battered on the rocks?"

"Well, I'd have some oars, of course," Seán protested. The young priest eyed the old man's stringy arms.

"Would you use canvas or does your celebration of ancient Celtic ingenuity require skin like Saint Brendan's?"

"Skin is the older way, but for my Callum's sake I'll use canvas. The lad cried when we gutted fish. He lost his stomach entirely any time we butchered a sheep . . ." He knit his brow, remembering. He'd felt so angry and called the boy soft, when he handed him the still bloody ram's hide to hang across the stone wall. Very sensitive he was about animals and killing. Wouldn't eat a thing for the rest of that day. Wouldn't again eat mutton after that. One night, the boy had even told his poor mother that her stew smelt of death and suffering. *Nonsense*, he'd called it back then. *He had no patience for boys who wouldn't eat good food when it was offered to them* and sent him to bed without supper. Seán blinked the memory out of mental sight and shook his head. "No, we'll use canvas. We'll coat it well in tar to seal it."

"And what material for the frame?"

"Larch is best, I think, for gunwales, seats, and thwarts. Supple and strong. Hazel for the ribs. Either larch or pine for the stringers—though back in Saint Brendan's time it would have been willow rods. Mine will be traditional in spirit at least, if not down to every detail. I've got my own ideas as well for this boat."

"I see, I see . . . well, you seem to know what you're about. Have you had any letter from your son yet? Any news of his whereabouts?" Father Martin always asked this with that terrible, irritating sweetness that Seán was learning to ignore.

"No, not as yet. But any day now, I know I'll be hearing from him. There's plenty of time if we aim to leave at some point in April or May. June at the latest, but May should be perfect. Most of the traveling birds should be back and nesting by then, or so your books tell me. Callum will want to see them and all their muddy little cliffside nests. And there's an island called Bass off of Scotland, just a rock, really, but hundreds of thousands of gannets nest on it. My Callum never did like the gannets as much as the other seabirds. Said they were a depraved lot. But I can't imagine he wouldn't want to see that many in one place. I'll wait on the construction until I do hear from him, though. I want us to build this boat together, you see."

And Father Martin did see. He smiled kindly at the old man's plans and wishes, but in his mind, he was troubled with memories of his own. In a way, he found that he envied this old fisherman's son whose father was trying so hard to find him. Wishing so fervently to make amends and making such extravagant plans for the adventure they would take together. He wondered if his own father . . . but it wasn't worth speculating about things he could never know. Still, this mad venture surprised him with hope—a bizarre and senseless hope that made him smile in spite of all his misgivings.

5

Tongues continued to wag in the village that early December when the strange parcels began to show up on the priory doorstep. Oddly shaped parcels arriving by special delivery addressed not to Father Martin but to Seán. One bulky bundle was stained with stinky black smears. Was the man paving a road on the island? There never had been a paved road on Thréig, but Seán was pretty old to be trying to build one himself with nothing but a shovel. And whatever would he want a paved road for anyway?

Then there were the long heavy bundles of lumber and hazel boughs that took two delivery men to carry. All of these mysterious materials were piling up at the priory along the garden wall, and poor Mrs. Kelly had been left with no instruction about what she was to do with them. Father Martin wasn't due back from Cork for another few days still. Another of those trips of his to visit his mother. He was meant to be back before the Feast of the Immaculate Conception, and hopefully no one would die in his absence this time. No one had the ambition to row out to Thréig and tell Seán to come and fetch his parcels from the priory, so they sat there by the wall in a heap. Mrs. Kelly finally threw a tarpaulin over them to at least keep the gray winter squalls from ruining them until the priest returned from Cork and took care of them himself.

When Father Martin did finally arrive back home in time for the start of the Christmas season, it was many a curious eye that watched with interest as he and Seán hauled these mysterious items to Sean's fishing boat and rowed them over to Thréig together. Was Father Martin helping Seán build his road? He *was* an advanced, progressive sort of priest, they thought, though why an island only one mile across with one permanent resident needed a paved road at all was anyone's guess. And all that lumber must be for something else, then.

The two men made several trips back and forth across to Thréig until the heap of parcels was gone and life went back to normal. At least the view from the various adjacent cottage windows went back to normal. Seán kept coming to visit the priest most days, which had *become* normal, but the event was not forgotten. Although no one could bring themselves to ask about it, for fear of Seán's powerful ill-wishing, it was generally agreed that the fisherman and the priest were up to something.

In the week before Christmas, the village began to bustle with young families arriving to spend the holiday with grandparents and great-grandparents. Seán appeared less frequently. The presence of strangers in the village made him uneasy since tales of his wicked exploits only grew in the re-telling.

"Is that the old man who did evil magic at Great-Auntie Maeve?" he'd heard a very young holiday visitor whisper too loudly in the post office, as he sent a fresh stack of enquiries to Dublin. Someone shushed the child, and Seán quickly made his way to the door without looking at the faces, though he knew they were all watching him.

Seán longed to be building the boat, busying his hands with planing long strips of larch, and knotting twine, and hammering tacks. He longed to be moving forward with his plans, instead of this *waiting*. It seemed he was cursed to a life in which he was always waiting for something. He'd taken to spending the long December evenings drawing up alternate designs and ideas for the boat, and visiting the old vacant sheep shed where he had used to keep ewes after difficult lambing. He hadn't kept any sheep at all for some time now. Not since he had been caring for Muireann. Her care, the fishing, and the garden was all he could manage on his own and he'd sold the remaining sheep at a loss. The shed now sat conveniently vacant for keeping his materials dry. He visited them in order to look them over, run his hands over the wood grain, and breathe in the spicy scent of lumber and tar. *Soon,* he would whisper to them, as much as to himself. *Soon.*

The afternoon of Christmas Eve was gray and chill. Seán sat with Finn warming his lap by the fire. Whenever he sat down now, Finn would soon be up on his lap purring raucously. He was growing heavier and more noble looking every day. Seán scratched under Finn's chin as the cat stretched out his neck, bunched up his lips, and narrowed his eyes into long contented slits.

"She loved Christmas, you know. Always wanted to go to the midnight mass, hear the *In Splendoribus Sanctorum,* take communion, and light

candles. Celebrate the miraculous birth," Seán said to the cat. He closed his own eyes now and pictured what it would be like to walk into the church this Christmas Eve alone. To sit by himself at the back where he mightn't be noticed. To hear the mass and sing the songs, to take the fleshly wafer if he dared—maybe light a candle for her. In his mind he went through the motions of it, removing his cap and smoothing his hair and making the sign of the cross.

You lost your only son as well, he said to the Virgin on the wall. *Sure, but he came back from the grave. Pray mine comes back to me . . . wherever he is.*

In the sanctuary of his mind, Seán rose and lit a candle, watching it flicker for a moment behind the red glass.

Pray mine comes back to me.

Then he would turn around and walk back to his currach in the darkness. He would untie it and row back to Thréig, even as the bells rang out at midnight through the frosty air, the much-anticipated miraculous birth.

He rowed and rowed into the black night and the cold. He rowed without light to guide him. He rowed until dawn when he ran aground on the shore of nowhere, heaving the currach up the shingle. He pressed himself, squeezed himself around the corner of his mind and into the best Christmas.

She had been ill and sleeping off and on that day. They had missed the midnight mass for the first time in their life together. She was pregnant with Callum and the first several weeks had been difficult for her. He lay next to her stroking her black seaweed hair when she suddenly jerked her head around and looked at him over her shoulder with wide, disbelieving eyes. She reached for his hand and placed it on her belly. They lay still for a moment, waiting, and then finally he felt it. He felt Callum for the first time that Christmas. They lay still and reveled in the glory of their own miracle. And as Seán lingered in this memory, it struck him how much it had felt like a small captive bird, fluttering its wings under the weight of his hand, trying even then, to fly away.

Evening was darkening the cottage when he opened his eyes. No. He would not go to Mass alone that night. He could not bear it without her. Finn chortled in annoyance as Seán lifted him from his lap and he stood, putting the cat down in the warm spot where he'd been sitting. He fumbled in a drawer of odds and ends—short pencils, odd nails, and scraps of paper until he found a tall candle. At least he would light a *Coinneal Mór na*

Nollag in the window. Muireann always used to. He remembered a time when every cottage on Thréig had had a great Christmas candle in its window on this night to welcome anyone in need of shelter, like the holy family themselves that night in Bethlehem. Now he was the only one left to keep the tradition.

He struck a match and held it to the wick. As it caught and glowed against the pane, he saw a face in the window. A wretched, lonely, withered face looking in at him as though searching for some little comfort from the cold. It startled him and he stared into the mournful eyes that stared back into his own. But it was only his own face reflected on the glass and he turned away from it.

6

As the New Year gradually washed away the tide of holiday visitors to the village, Seán ventured back to the priory with his collection of drawings and plans. He told himself he needed to see if Father Martin had brought back any new books from Cork, but he also felt a strange urge to show another person his ideas for the sailing currach. Seán spread his drawings out on Father Martin's desk as they ate leftover cradle-shaped Christmas pies.

"This is she, Father. Not the sort of boat your Pa will have known in the coast guard by any stretch. But you know, I think you might like this one better. It's much more like those old poems that you just sort of feel. Sure, there's rules to make a boat float just as there's rules to make your different sorts of poems work, but there's a lot of room for a mind to play, and that's where the pleasure of it lies."

"Well, you're right, there. It's nothing like the boat my father captained. I'm afraid it doesn't look very safe, though. Not for the open ocean," Father Martin said, brushing pastry crumbs off the front of his cassock.

"Now, Father, there've been currachs in Ireland for as long as we know, and it got our saintly ancestors safe to the Scottish Islands, to Rome . . . and all the way to the shores of North America if you believe the tales of Saint Brendan."

"Those tales probably aren't factual, Seán. Can you imagine meeting icebergs in an open skin craft? It would tear the boat to shreds and you'd freeze to death in minutes. They're grand stories, but that's probably all they are. Best to read it as a legend with a grain of truth—the truth in it being a spiritual kind. Don't go following Saint Brendan into dangers even he never faced."

"Ah, but holy missions are blessed with the kind of boldness that laughs in the face of freezing seas and like dangers."

"Still, my son," Father Martin said with his blazing smile and terrible sweetness, "a detailed boat plan and a little preparation never hurt a holy mission."

"Well, you'll be hard pressed to find *detailed* plans ready drawn up for a currach of any size. It's a layman's vessel built to your own tastes and needs. There's regional differences as well. My father always gave his a bit of a pointy, turned up nose. No reason I could tell at the time except that he liked the look of it. But it can also have a gentle curve from front to back or shoot straight across like your faster currachs for calmer waters and loughs. Though it's not just for looks that you'd turn up a currach's prow. She can handle waves better that way, and as I'm heading to open ocean, I want a boat that can handle the waves . . . what's the matter, Father?"

"I just—I thought you had a pretty clear idea of dimensions when we talked about it last. I thought you must have since you had all your supplies delivered already. I had no idea the boat you were building was so . . . subjectively proportioned. What if you find you've not got enough of something?"

"Sure, it'll be fine. When it comes to holy missions, you'll find at the last minute that you always have enough—though seldom more than exactly your need. And in that spirit, I have decided that if I begin to build the boat, my Callum will come. Yes . . . if I step forward in faith and begin the work, I have no doubt that one of my letters will find my boy and fetch him straight here to me. I'll start tomorrow, in fact. You know, you could come over, Father . . . it could be interesting for you to see how a *traditional* currach is built, before they all go extinct with men like me."

Seán had judged well the focus of this subtle appeal for Father Martin's help. It was his interest in ancient Irish history, language, and culture that had brought the young priest to that remote corner of the Gaeltacht to begin with. He had not grown up speaking the Irish language at home and while his was what might be considered a privileged upbringing, it was in some ways culturally impoverished. After a school trip to Inis Cealtra during his teenage years, the future priest had taken an interest in the ancient Celtic Saints and Church history—specifically its role in the spiritual and cultural formation of this complex and turbulent land. His interest grew to include all things classified as endemically Irish, and he suffered the painful beginnings of a deep-seated resentment that no one had thought it important to speak Irish to him as a child or tell him any of the old stories. Therefore, the

invitation to observe and potentially assist in the building of a traditional currach proved irresistible to Father Martin.

"I suppose I could lend a hand . . . if you like," Father Martin said, pretending to examine his fingernails, though inwardly leaping up and down like an excited child.

"Fine. Come early. I'll meet you by the shrine and we'll walk up to the cottage together."

7

T HE SUN HADN'T YET risen that frosty January morning when Father Martin pulled his rowboat close to the dock at the little eastern port of Thréig, confident he would be there before Seán. They hadn't set an exact time, after all, but as Father Martin approached, there was the old fisherman paying his respects to the Virgin nestled into her grotto in the rock face.

"Have you been here long?" Father Martin called to him as he tossed the old man his dripping rope.

"Not long. No more than an hour," Seán said cheerfully tying the rope to a piling with expert swiftness.

"I'm sorry to have kept you waiting. I thought I'd be arriving well before you."

"It's no trouble at all—I was up early. There's something in the air this morning, isn't there, Father? You can *smell* Time! You can just smell it in the air . . . and it's full! We've important work before us."

"Lead on," Father Martin said with the smile of a parent humoring an excited child, though inwardly he felt the same sense of significance floating on the breeze from the cold, churning winter sea. Something extraordinary could happen on a morning like this.

The two walked along in silence through the chill, blue dawn. A mist lay over the lumpy green land in wisps and swirls. They walked through boggy swales past the lough, squelching through patches of black mud that threatened to suck off Father Martin's galoshes. They spied glaucous gulls sleeping along the banks of the lough, unbothered by their passing, even when the priest yelped loudly in dismay after leaving his whole shoe in its ineffectual rubber sheath behind him in the mud.

When the sun finally crested the horizon, its golden rays flamed the mist that lay sparkling all about them like a veil clinging to the weather-beaten grass, hovering there and not there. Real and not real. The air was

murmurous with voices of seabirds, and the two men were shorn of all practical care and rage at the squelching *greallach* in the radiance of that morning.

"Lord have mercy!" Father Martin exclaimed, making the sign of the cross and leaving his hand resting on his heart. "Such a sight finds me quite unworthy!"

Seán laughed. And people wondered why he wanted to stay on the island, hemmed in by capricious seaways that assured his separate destiny. They only needed to see it—really see it, in all its glory and its terror to understand how an island takes ownership of the souls that love it.

"Here we are," Seán said as at last he led the way to the familiar dry-stone wall, where Finn sat upright waiting for him like a staring stone gargoyle.

"Is that you Finn? You've grown up a bit since last I saw you. I wouldn't know you're the same creature," Father Martin exclaimed.

Seán smiled as Finn stood up on his hind legs to meet his descending hand with the top of his head.

"He wanted to survive, it turns out," he said, the corners of his mouth twisting upward. Finn closed his yellow eyes in ecstasy under the heavy, stroking hand and purred in great thundering gusts. Then Seán clapped both hands and rubbed them together with a distinct twinkle in his eye. "Right, so Father! I will make the shape here first and we'll get started."

The priest watched as Seán took some chalk and sketched out the rough A-frame outline of a boat on the grass—measuring the length and width with his own boots from heel to toe. He sat himself down on the grass in the middle of the chalk outline and nodded in approval.

"That's about right, I think." Finn came arching his back, mincing, and rubbing up against Seán as he sat there, frost melting and seeping into his trousers. He began considering how he would get up again without creaking, tottering, and moving the young priest to unbearable acts of compassion. How seaworthy would he seem if he couldn't even get himself back up on his own? Seán improvised by inviting the priest to come and sit in the chalk outline with him, "for a sense of scale with two men aboard, you understand."

"Ah . . . where do you want me?"

"Up there in her throat—toward the bow, Father if you please. That's where I see Callum sitting. Let me just get a feel for how it fits two with

supplies for a journey." Father Martin sat where he was told, cross-legged, facing Seán awkwardly.

"No, no—not like that, Father. You'll not see any rocks ahead if you're facing me."

"Oh, sorry," he said scooching himself around to face what should be the way ahead. As Father Martin raised a theatrical hand to his brow, and declared no dangerous rocks in their immediate path, Seán rolled himself onto all fours and heaved himself up with some crackling and creaking of joints before the priest turned back around. When Father Martin looked back at Seán, the old man displayed a strong and powerful stance, hands on his hips, and the gray cat bending and wrapping itself around his leg.

"Yes, this looks about right to me," he said with a nod, and beckoned the priest to follow him to the sheep shed where he had kept his lumber dry. Father Martin, inhibited slightly by his cassock, labored gracelessly to his own feet to follow while Seán charitably averted his gaze.

"So, how do we start, then?" Father Martin asked, brushing off his now damp cassock and following Seán to the sheep shed.

"The frame. We know the shape and more or less the size we want. It's a basic A-frame, that means it's pointy at the nose and squared off at the back, you know" he explained, as though to a very small child. "Gunwales and thwarts are all part of one structure—rigid." Seán picked up a sawhorse, gestured for Father Martin to take the other, and carried them to the chalk outline. We'll shape the larch, fasten it together with stainless steel bolts and bands for extra support. I know, stainless steel isn't traditional, but I'm old and it gives me peace of mind."

So, the two of them set to work, Seán doing most of the cutting and planing and bolting while Father Martin held things and fetched things and tried not to be in the way. Finn played around their feet, swatting at falling wood shavings and sneezing. He tried to climb up under Father Martin's cassock, to the priest's dismay, leaving sprinklings of clinging silver hairs in his wake.

"So, your father taught you to do this when you were a boy?" Father Martin asked.

"I mostly watched back then. He liked doing things himself. I had my own ideas about boats that he didn't quite like."

"Oh? You wanted to try some modern techniques, did you?"

"Not at all. If anything, I wanted something even more ancient. I was always wanting to make a great big skin currach with a sail like Saint

Brendan's. Something to tack out to sea in and go adventuring and discovering new lands. But there haven't been skin currachs since the 1820s or so, and my father wouldn't have any of it."

"Your father wouldn't have a skin currach or a son off having adventures?"

"Neither. A very practical man, my father. Efficient. Forceful. Not much patience for little boys with fanciful ambitions."

"Sounds a bit like mine," Father Martin mused.

"A hard man is your father?"

"Mmmm—quite."

"Proud of you though, I'd guess. Becoming a priest and all that."

Father Martin laughed and shook his head.

"Quite the opposite, I assure you."

"What? Not proud of all your learning and your good works? I doubt that."

"There can be no doubt, I'm afraid. I took the name of Martin at my baptism for a reason."

"What? Were you not baptized as an infant?"

"No, my father wouldn't hear of it. Violently opposed to religion, like Saint Martin's."

"Martin of Tours, is it?"

"The same. He disobeyed his father, too, you see. My father wasn't simply indifferent to religion. As he saw it, all of Ireland's troubles throughout history had been in some way caused or at least exacerbated by religion. It was the root of all social unrest, political turmoil, and violent conflict—a land torn both physically and figuratively between England and Rome. I was only ever baptized at all because I attended catechism secretly when I was sixteen. I came to it on my own when I learned of the ancient Celtic church and its saints. When I told him I was to enter the priesthood . . . well . . . "

"He couldn't have been too pleased, I suppose."

"You could say that. My father, atheist though he was, felt his pagan roots most keenly when he'd taken drink, and at those times, he could summon all those forces of darkness he didn't believe in over the slightest offense. He'd had a few when I told him—but by then there was hardly a time of the day when his brains weren't a bit curdled with drink, so no time would have suited any better. I told him I wanted something different—that he might see religion as the cause of all Ireland's troubles, and surely it has

played its role, but I thought healing was to be found in the spiritual beauty of our past and our saints. Well, his face turned purple, and the vein stood out on his forehead, and he started flinging every curse he could think of."

"He cursed his own son?"

"Oh yes! Quite a range, from itches I wouldn't be able to reach to a terrible death at sea.

Seán dropped his block plane and stared aghast.

"And here you are rowing out over the sea to my island. Aren't you frightened to set food in a boat?"

Father Martin laughed.

"The powers of evil can't touch me unless God wills it. He cursed me, true enough, but it wasn't to death at sea."

"What do you mean?"

"He cursed me to *life* knowing that my own father was so ashamed of me as to wish me suffering and death. That was his curse. And if you think of it, there's really no more appalling notion than that, is there?"

"He regretted it," Seán said in a low, quiet voice. "I'm sure he regretted it the moment he said it and just couldn't tell you . . . for pride. No father truly wishes any harm or pain for his own child, no matter the differences between them. But pride . . . the devil's own vice . . . I'm sure . . . I know he regretted it terribly. Regrets it still and thinks of it when he can't sleep at night. Wishes he could take it all back. I'm sure of it."

"You may be right, but I'll never know. We never spoke again, you see. My father died suddenly of a heart attack not long after I left."

Seán crossed himself.

"And here I was thinking you were too young to have ever lost anyone. Does it hurt you terribly, still?"

"I still hurt, but for *him*—for the burden of anger he lived with in his last years. I don't hurt for myself now. I don't doubt the path I took. I wish we could have been reconciled, though. It's a sore spot in a man's heart to know he hasn't got his own father's blessing."

"Yes . . . I fear it is," Seán said slowly with a catch in his voice. "But you forgave *him*. You forgave your father without him asking you even, and I'm sure knowing that would have given him peace. No father with any natural feeling in him speaks that way to his child without the weight of regret hanging on him like a great stone around his neck. Poor man . . . *poor man!*" Seán crossed himself again and stared hard at the trampled grass beneath his feet. His scalp felt as though it were on fire despite the

cold of the morning, and his stomach churned. Yet, he felt also a distinct softening toward the young priest. Father Martin sighed and bent to pick up the block plane that Seán had dropped. He handed it to the old man, a vague smile escaping slowly across his young pink face.

"Could I have a go with that, do you think, Seán? Watching the way the wood comes off in those curls . . . it must be one of the most beautiful and satisfying things I've ever seen in my life! Who would have thought such a small, simple thing could bring such joy."

Seán smiled at this and understood.

"Of course, son, er . . . Father."

8

"MAMMY, WHY DID SAINT Columcille have to leave Ireland?"

"Well, the story I've most often heard is that of the Cathach and the troubles that came from it."

"What's the Cathach?"

"The Cathach is the earliest ecclesiastical manuscript produced in Ireland. It's attributed to our Saint Columcille—a book of psalms. But it's also a book that caused a lot of problems."

"What sorts of problems?"

"Pride, Callum. Like a great many of the problems between men, then as now, pride was likely at its root. Did you know that in the time of Saint Columcille, it was very rare to be able to read or write? When the Roman Empire fell, the ancient libraries were destroyed along with the wisdom they contained. The old books were forgotten along with the skill to make sense of them. Reading became so rare a skill that it was like magic!"

"Magic!"

"Yes, like magic, being able to look at strange scratches and squiggles on a rock or a piece of parchment and make meaning out of them. But what was even more magical was being able to produce new meanings of your own in that way. Saint Columcille was one of those few people who could make words—mere scritches and scratches on a page—come to life! Some have said that as a child he was fed a cake with all the letters of the alphabet baked into it, and so he came to love writing because of that strange alphabet cake inside him."

"That's silly."

"It's just a story. We know that it was his monastery schooling and wise, learned masters who taught him how to read and write. He read the old histories and poems of Ireland, and even wrote some of his own. He was what they called in those days a *scribe.*"

"Like scribble?"

"Like scribble, but his scribbles were beautiful and full of deep meanings. He loved reading, but in those days, there were not very many books available to him. His old master, Saint Finnian had something very rare and special in his possession, though. Do you remember what it was? Something he brought back with him from his trip to Rome."

"The Holy Scriptures?"

"That's right. And Saint Columcille wanted to make a nice copy of it. If he could but have his way, he would make a copy for every one of the monasteries and churches he'd founded by then, so that each may have those words to read and ponder. But Saint Finnian said no."

"Why?"

"Saint Finnian liked owning a book that was the only one of its kind. He took pride in how rare and fine it was and didn't want anyone making copies of it, for he felt that diminished the value of his original. But Saint Columcille wouldn't take no for an answer and decided that he would secretly make that copy anyway. Copying a book in those days was no easy task. There wouldn't be printing presses for another thousand years nor even paper to write on, at least not like what we use today. Any book at the time would have been written by hand with a quill pen and ink made from plants and minerals on parchment made from animal skin scraped smooth and thin. It was a long and laborious undertaking, just to make the materials, not to mention the actual inscription."

"What if you made a mistake?"

"Well, maybe that's why there were little swirls and designs and birds and things on the old manuscripts. Maybe they were wee mistakes that the scribes turned into decorations, and then the decorations became great works of art. Maybe. I don't know. I'm sure there is some sort of lesson in that if you look for it. But every night while the brothers of the monastery slept, Saint Columcille would sneak into the scriptorium to work on his copy of Saint Finnian's book. He settled on copying down only the psalms, for copying the scriptures in their entirety would take more time than he had. Eventually, Saint Columcille finished his beautiful copy and, of course, Saint Finnian found out."

"What did Saint Finnian do?"

"Well, he was that angry, wasn't he! He said that since the original was his, and this new copy wouldn't have existed without it, that both books should belong to him by rights. Saint Columcille said that the copy should

belong to himself because he had done all the hard work to make it, and anyway, Saint Finnian already had his own. Finally, Diarmait, the High King at Tara, heard both of their claims and decided that Saint Finnian should have the copy that Saint Columcille had made."

"But why? If Saint Columcille did all the work!"

"The king said, 'to every cow her calf.' Since Brehon Law at the time would have given Saint Finnian the calf if he owned the cow, he determined that the copy, which he considered to be the offspring of the original book, should stay with the original owner."

"Books aren't the same as cows!"

"No, they're not. But that was Diarmait's ruling. Even saints are under authority, and this would prove to be a great test for our saint. Whether it was fair or not, Saint Columcille lost his case, and he was none too happy about it. It was a shame, really. You remember that pride and a tendency toward anger were crosses he bore in life? Well, it was at this time that he faced those tendencies in himself with the most tragic outcome. His clan was proud and powerful as were his friends, and they were all insulted along with Saint Columcille. They decided to wage war."

"War! Over a book?"

"Over a book, but also over their honor. To insult one member of their clan was to insult them all. It was terrible. Many men died in the ensuing battle, but the Hy Nialls won. Yes . . . they won the battle, and Saint Columcille's honor may have been defended and his hard work recovered, but at what cost? How could a monk live a worthy life with so much blood on his hands? He was ordered to appear before an ecclesiastical council of Ireland's most holy fathers to receive their censure for stirring up strife. For even though the King's ruling may have been unjust, it is for servants of Christ to bear injustice with patience, rather than to seek vengeance through bloodshed. This realization smote Saint Columcille to the heart, and he cried out 'Against Thee only have I sinned and done this evil in Thy sight: For I acknowledge my fault, and my sin is ever before me.'

"His conscience ached with the sincerity of repentance, and the council gave their sentence: that for every man fallen on the field of battle because of him, Columcille must convert one pagan soul to Christ. From the depths of our saint's repentance, this seemed too lenient a penance, and he sought the counsel of his friend, Saint Molaise to help guide him to find a more fitting penance. Realizing that Saint Columcille's love for his own country and his own clan and his desire for earthly justice had encroached

on his love of God and mankind, it was decided that the most appropriate penance would be for him to complete his task in another land—that he should live in exile from his own beloved Ireland and its people, and never look upon his homeland again.

"Saint Columcille must atone for his actions through prayer and fasting in the wild, desolate islands of the Hebrides among the Druids. So, he and twelve companions from the monastery at Daire took their big wicker currach wrapped in ox hide, out to sea for the perilous journey north."

"How did he know where to go, and how far?"

"The Norse Gaels had sailed up from the coasts of Ireland to the Hebrides for some time before. He knew well what he would find if he set out to the land of forests and its islands of the western seas. In a day's sailing they landed at Oronsay, but he would not settle on any island where he could still see his native land, even distantly, so they sailed on northward. Finally, Saint Columcille and his twelve friends reached Iona, and this was where they decided to build their monastery. They constructed little bee-hive shaped cells there on that wild, bleak, and rocky island and struggled to live worthy lives and to spread Christianity to Scotland."

"So, he didn't copy books anymore?"

"He did! But I'd guess he made sure to have permission first after that bad scene with Saint Finnian! They built a scriptorium at the monastery on Iona and produced beautiful manuscripts that were not only illuminated with fanciful designs but illuminating to a world that had nearly lost all of its books and the stories they held. And it is through stories that we remember who we are, Callum. They remind us that we're human and that we're not alone."

"I don't want to be a human! I'd rather be a bird!"

"Wouldn't we all, my darling! It's such a burden to be human . . . but a blessing too. You aren't bound to the law of instinct—the harsh law of tooth and claw as animals are. You can choose. You can show compassion, love, and forbearance even when it's not deserved. You can struggle against instinct and passion to do what's right rather than what's easy. You can show mercy. You can forgive. A bird can't make peace with a fox in this world. But two men who live as enemies can make peace with one another and become friends. That's one of the blessings of humanity—the ability to forgive and be forgiven."

"I'd still rather be able to fly."

"You feel that way now. You might not always."

* * *

"Ribs today, Father," Seán said as he met the priest again at the little shrine by the dock.

"I'm ready!" Father Martin said with his broad and blinding smile.

"I hope so for your sake. It's a lot of knots you'll be tying today. Fixing the ribs is a two-man job anyway, but I need your nimble young fingers. Mine have suffered a bit with arthritis these past few years."

"How many knots do you mean?"

"Oh, a good four hundred at least, for a smaller currach. That's traditional. But this one will take more."

"That many! Will we get it all done today even?"

"Well, if not, we'll at least break the back of it."

The two walked side by side the now familiar path to Seán's cottage. Father Martin wore a new pair of tall rubber boots this time, which still sucked and squelched in the mud, but at least spared his good shoes. The currach's frame had been kept dry in the sheep shed and Seán had it set up on the sawhorses to continue working on it in shelter from the clawing winter wind and the sudden unpredictable bursts of winter rain.

"You've drilled holes in the gunwales?"

"That's where the ribs will fit in. Today we need to shape these hazel boughs so the ends will fit into the holes. Two boughs will stretch across from one side to the other and meet in the middle. That's where we secure them with your good knots once we've bent and shaped them right."

"How do you know how long each rib piece ought to be? And how tightly bent?"

"By sight. We'll know it's right because it will *look* right."

"In my experience as a priest, sometimes things look right enough, but they're really all wrong. There's how things look and how things are. They rarely match up."

"People and boats are different, Father. A man can hide his sorrows and his sins behind a smile—choose words that soften his wrongdoings in the confessional—but there's nothing hidden when it comes to currachs. You can trust your own eyes to know if you've done it right."

"How refreshing. If only everything in life were that straightforward."

The two men were glad of the sheep shed when the rain started. The first gentle patterings filled the silence so that their minds could settle on the work in front of them rather than searching for things to say. The patterings

grew to a *clagarnach* as the rain spit down, clanging the iron roof, but in the shelter of the shed they pressed on in their careful work. Slowly, with the addition of each corresponding hazel rib, the currach's shape began to form—tapered at the bow, then swelling smoothly outward in a full-figured curve.

"It's like a creature, isn't it? A man could lie in the bottom of a currach and nearly believe he was in the belly of a great fish, like Jonah!" Father Martin mused, examining their work while rubbing his sore, red fingers.

Seán nodded.

"You know, it's odd you say that, Father. My Callum was always going on about Jonah, and the great fish that swallowed him. He even told me more than once that *he* ought to have been named Jonah, though he'd never say why."

"But he *was* named after Jonah," Father Martin said with a grin.

"How do you mean?"

"Well, Callum means Dove."

"I know that . . . and Columcille is Dove of the Church."

"Yes, exactly. But what do you think Jonah means in the Hebrew?"

9

E VEN WITH WORK FOR his hands to do and a worthy goal before him, Seán's mind at rest was prone to these sudden gusts of memory. Sudden visions of the way light slanted through the bedroom window illuminating dust motes like plankton, the special little jiggle one had to give the door handle, or that one squeaky floorboard in the hall. The lengths he went to trying to tread lightly around that particular board so as not to wake her on his way out. How many mornings had he woken to the sound of the sea and the birds and her breathing? When his mind was still waking, and his open eyes didn't see the room yet, but still saw the dream rising and falling like waves.

How many times had he blinked through shifting scenes of sleep to that reality. That bedroom. That crack in the ceiling. That unlit oil lamp. That square pane of blue dawn with raindrops slithering down distorted panes. The nest she'd made of her pillow with dark curls spilling over the side. Her shoulder rising like an island, sloping down to her waist then up again at the hip. A living, breathing island rising from the sea of blue and white quilt, the pillow's shore streaming with black seaweed. How it had struck him in those moments that she really was an island. An island he could never fully know—for so much of an island is hidden beneath the sea. But that part which he knew, he had loved. Those protean shapes had been the reality, sharpening with the retreating tide of dream. Now they had become the dream itself from which he reluctantly woke. But he knew even when he was in them that the dreams were a drug—a temporary relief not to be over-indulged—otherwise, he might never wake from them, and he must wake. He had a reason now.

Seán gently, dutifully tore an opening in the thin web separating these two worlds and pushed himself through to waking. He heaved himself up from his chair as the last wisps of dream fled like fog in sunlight. Those

memories were a way of keeping her, if only while the dream lasted, and this had been one of his best. How remarkable it is that the memory of a moment should be so much richer than the moment itself when it happens. It must be the lifetime that follows the moment which creates the meaning and gives it shape.

Finn scrunched up his face as he stretched. He purred loudly, nipping at the old man's calf demanding his breakfast. The early February sun hadn't yet risen when Seán stepped out into the garden. A salty mist hovered over the grass like a spirit. In that murky half-light, he saw a dark shape moving noiselessly through the mist near the old sheep shed. He walked cautiously toward it, gripping the stick which he had grown accustomed to using on his walks down the cliff.

As Seán drew near, a man's form—tall and young, quite thin, but Seán suspected, quite strong, grew in clarity through the mist. What young stranger was lurking on his island at this hour? He gripped his stick tighter and raised it against his shoulder at the ready. He could just make out a shabby pair of trousers and an oversized wool sweater that hung from high, slightly hunched shoulders. Seán's heart took flight, and he threw the stick down onto the dewy grass.

Running toward the sheep shed through the veil of mist, Seán cried out, "Callum! Callum!" and held out his arms toward the specter. The young man turned toward his calls and Seán's heart seemed to stop with a sickening flutter.

"No, Seán—no, it's only myself," Father Martin's voice called out. The old man stumbled and just caught himself from falling to his knees in the wet, squashy grass. This was never Father Martin; he was surely hallucinating. Perhaps he was still in his armchair asleep by the fire with Finn on his lap, and this was all some vivid dream. The man would soon sprout feathers and fly as in the others. Seán strained his eyes against the shifting, grainy obscurity of the mist and the murk.

"Who is this apparition in my garden, speaking with Father Martin's voice in my own boy's clothes?" The man walked over to Seán. Even his posture and stride—long and lanky with the slight spring of youth—was so very like Callum, but the face that appeared out of the mist was the young priest's.

"I'm sorry to startle you, Seán. I arrived earlier so as to spare you the walk down to meet me."

"I thought . . .you looked just like . . ."

97

"My cassock has proven impractical for this sort of work. I hope you don't mind. I suppose you've never seen me out of it before."

"I just . . . I never realized how like you are to my Callum. Seeing you like this . . . I thought my boy had come back, that's all."

"I understand. I'm sorry to have given you such a fright. Would you like to go back inside for a few moments? You're white as a sheet and quaking too."

The priest led Seán back inside and sat him down shaking in his armchair. Father Martin put the kettle on, then the two men fell to silently examining each other over steaming mugs of tea. Father Martin watched Seán for signs of physical distress. He knew a severe fright could lead to such things as heart attacks in those predisposed and watched the rise and fall of the old man's chest as if the watching and willing hard enough might prevent such an incident. He fingered a string of beads wrapped thrice around his wrist.

Seán kept examining the young priest's person in disbelief. Folded up nearly in half as he was in Muireann's chair, the young priest, absent of cassock or priestly vestment, seemed just a boy—a boy who needed a new pair of trousers and better-fitting sweater before going off to Dublin without even a fatherly blessing to warm his heart. Those hunched shoulders that always seemed embarrassed of their height, and even the large but gentle hands resting on high, sharp knees. The chair was meant for a small woman, not a tall lad. Was this what Seán had driven his own boy to as well? Was Callum off building a boat and a friendship with someone else's father—a better father who was telling him how well he'd done and how proud he should be? He pictured his boy with his paragon of fatherly virtue and ground his teeth with bitter shame and jealousy.

Father Martin mistook this sudden tooth grinding for a sign of pain, and stared harder at Seán's chest, willing the heart within to beat strong and steady with the prayers of the Mother of God and all the saints shoring up his own. He had not prayed enough for his own father, in spite of having forgiven him. He had not prayed enough, and his father had died of a heart attack. The young priest's brow knit with concentration such that Seán thought he was impatient to be working on the boat. He drank down his tea too quickly, burning his tongue and the roof of his mouth. He rose tearing his eyes away from the young man folded up in Muireann's chair like a sheet of rumpled paper.

"I'm all right now, Father. You startled me is all. I'll light us a lantern and we can make a start on the stringers."

"Stringers?" Father Martin echoed dreamily, finally tearing his own eyes away from Seán's chest.

"Stringers. Long strips of larch running from front to back of the boat to keep the canvas off the frame and give fullness to the shape. It's a big job. Hundreds more knots for you to tie."

"So be it. We can sit longer if you need. There's no rush."

"There is, though. I've waited long enough. Far too long if I'm honest."

10

THE STRINGERS TOOK WEEKS as Seán carefully measured, shaped, and sanded each long, thin strip of larch to fit over the framework of hazel ribs. With the start of Lent, Father Martin expected to be busy with liturgical activity, and had to shorten his time spent on Thréig in order to make himself available to the parish. As his soup suppers continued to be sparsely attended or unattended entirely, and his extended confession hours went quietly unheeded, the priest took to locking up early and rowing back over to Thréig. He would bring with him a large thermal flask of Mrs. Kelly's Lenten soup and a loaf of soda bread to share with Seán as they continued to place each strip until the currach looked like a proper boat instead of a large woven creel.

When the stringers were finally finished, they left the cold sheep shed and would sit by the peat fire in the cottage as Seán carefully shaped the canvas skin and sewed pieces together by hand with an awl and thick waxed thread. In this manner, February slipped into March, with Seán stitching and Father Martin sitting in Muireann's chair, stroking the now huge Finn who, if left unattended, would flump himself down on the canvas and stare accusingly at Seán for ignoring him. If they didn't remove him quickly, the great gray cat would begin picking at the weave of the canvas with his needle-sharp claws, his hind end raised in the air, front legs stretched out prickling before him, and tail lashing indignantly.

"Is this canvas thick enough, Seán?" Father Martin scooped Finn up and held him like a baby in the crook of one arm as the cat sulked and glowered. He felt the edge of the shaped fabric between the fingers of his free hand. "It doesn't seem like it would offer much strength, especially when one bored cat could shred it to ribbons given the chance."

"15 ounces—quite heavy enough. Remember it hasn't got tar on it yet."

"And the thread at the seams will hold once you've stretched it across?"

"Should."

"It just looks small for the frame. What if you can't stretch it enough to cover it . . . or if the seams pop open with the strain?"

"It'll fit. You'll see," Seán smiled confidently.

When the stitching and shaping was complete, they finally draped the finished canvas skin over the frame, covering its back and curving sides evenly like a rug over the steaming back of a plow-horse after a long day in the fields. Seán gripped a few brass tacks between pursed lips and held the edge of the skin in place at the gunwale before pounding them in a snug line across the first side. Father Martin mostly watched, handing Seán more brass tacks as he required them until the entire first side was fixed, and they moved on to the other.

The canvas fit smoothly over the stringers, a perfect fit that Seán further tightened by pounding the ribs down from their holes along the gunwales until the canvas stretched tight like the skin of a drum. He ran an admiring hand over the smooth creamy canvas before boiling the tar in a cauldron over a fire in the garden.

"Oh! It breaks my heart to see it get all smeared and smelly like that!" Father Martin moaned as Seán poured the bubbly black stuff all down the boat's upturned keel from bow to stern. "It was so beautiful and clean before."

"Beautiful and clean," Seán conceded, "but it wouldn't have floated. She's got to be sealed with a few coats to make her watertight. Here, take a brush and spread it—quickly now. We've got to cover every inch."

Father Martin brushed the tar across the taught skin of the currach along one side while Seán worked on the other. They did this twice and thrice before they finally took a step back, hands and trousers smeared and smelly with tar. She was sleek and black like a wet seal, basking on a sunny shore.

"Now we wait."

11

THE TAR WAS DRYING nicely as the currach rested in the old sheep shed that March. The mast was shaped and sanded smooth. It leaned against the wall as the currach dried, resting upturned on its gunwales. The halyard was constructed, ropes and pullies and sail all sat at the ready, clean, neatly folded, wound, and waiting. Father Martin arrived that morning to find Seán running his block plane down the length of an oar he was shaping out of larch. The final task, and this was almost finished too.

"I've brought you your mail, Seán. There's a letter from Dublin." Seán dropped the block plane and dusted off his hands before taking the letter from the priest. There had been others. Letters that bore nothing but the same message time and time again: that Callum was no longer there and had left no forwarding address, or that they did not know him at all. This time felt different, and Seán's hand, blackened with splatters of tar, trembled as he tore open the envelope.

Father Martin watched Seán's face as he read, waiting for the usual shrug, the usual resignation that he must simply keep on trying. But the old man's face remained an inscrutable blank. His face was blank even as his hand crumpled the letter bitterly in his dusty fist and bent to pick up the oar again. Blank even as he ran his hand slowly along the smooth haft of the oar. Blank as he rammed the oar with all his might and strength and passion into the heart of the beautiful black currach, like a harpoon into a whale, with a heart-rending crack.

"Seán!" Father Martin caught hold of the old man's arm. Seán's head filled with a swirling darkness, constellated with electric sparks flashing behind his shuttered eyes, and to his knees he fell, crumpled into the pile of wood curls and shavings that littered the earthen floor of the sheep shed. Father Martin wrapped a long arm around Seán's shoulders muttering, "Lord have mercy . . . Lord have mercy . . ." Seán gasped and buried his

face in calloused hands, convulsing with sobs he could no longer contain. They took him in great, rolling waves. These were tears that he had never shed for Muireann, even at her last breath. All the words between them had long been said, and he felt her death as an open sort of sorrow—open and somehow complete. Not closed-off and truncated like this.

"What's happened?" Father Martin asked at last, as the waves of sobs eased up. Seán stiffened, pulling away from the priest's arm, feeling the shame not only of his tears but of a lifetime of failures bearing down upon him with the weight of a thousand oceans. He drew in a breath and surveyed the currach's torn black skin.

"He's gone."

"Where? Where's he gone?"

"Dead, they say."

"What? What happened?"

"He was *honored* with a rare and prestigious research fellowship to study migratory birds—damn them! He was in Africa all through the fall and early winter. Last month, he was going around the Inner Hebrides on his own when he stopped radioing in. They've searched but found nothing, and now they've stopped looking for him altogether. He'll soon be declared dead, Father." Father Martin reached out to touch Seán's arm, but the old man recoiled. "They believe he was caught up in the strait of Corryvrecken—between Jura and Scarba. It's taken down many a small craft before, even when those at the helm were familiar with its wiles. That's around where he was meant to be."

"Jesus wept!" the priest exclaimed, crossing himself.

"This has all been for nothing. He's dead and this has all been for nothing. There never was a hope. It was just a distraction while I wait . . . I—I'm not strong enough for this, Father."

"You'll have to be. What other choice is there?"

Seán nodded and sniffed as he stared into the black hole punched into the currach's heart. They were both silent a moment, until Father Martin, in his still youthful simplicity said, "I find that tea is always a good decision. There are no downsides to it, and often it helps to clear the fog a little when the way forward is unclear." The young priest reached again toward Seán, a large, gentle young hand that rested on the old man's shoulder. Seán did not back away from it but nodded and turned his back on the wounded boat, walking slowly toward the empty cottage.

12

I T HAD BEEN A long time since anyone in the village had taken much notice of Father Martin. His reputation was firmly fixed as too "advanced"—too urban—too enthusiastic—and far, far too young. But when he started failing to show up for vespers . . . matins . . . confession . . . now, in the midst of Lent when a priest ought to be at the disposal of his parish, and he and his little boat were consistently absent, people began to sit up and take notice.

Had he given up? Had he reached the end of all that youthful optimism and lost interest in them altogether? Some of his parishioners began to feel positively jilted. Of course they did not wish to see him at confession, even if it *was* Lent, but they liked having the option all the same. Of course they hadn't the time or inclination to join him in that ridiculous society for the reading of edifying books, or his soup suppers, or the ill-fated community garden, but they liked seeing him pottering around the priory smiling— always smiling. That young man simply couldn't control his face. Perhaps someone ought to have given him a little encouragement. Not a lot, mind you, but enough to keep him trying. It was as if their prince had given up on his princess who had played just a little too hard to get and gone off to find someone more receptive to his attentions. They did not like it.

What's more, they did not like *where* Father Martin had gone. He was giving far too much of his time and priestly energies to the one last resident of Thréig to the exclusion of everyone else. And that one was a lost cause if ever there was one. What if they needed him here? Were they to row all the way out to the island to fetch him? Risk the caprices of the sea and Old Seán's powerful ill-wishings? A priest's place was in the priory—the church—and the "field of his labors," meaning the village.

Father Martin was not oblivious to the situation. He had long been conscious that his ministry was becoming limited to one parishioner, which

was quite clearly inappropriate. A good father cares for all his children, but he felt that of all his children there was one hurting more than the rest. One lonelier and more isolated. Many motives brought him to Seán's island day after day—some obvious and others less so. Perhaps he felt the old fisherman needed someone to care and to listen. Perhaps he really was interested in the endemic craft of currach building. Perhaps this father to the parish had need of a father himself. He knew his duty, though, and knew his days spent on Thréig were numbered. That being the case, he must use them as best he could.

* * *

But how had it come to this? You would think he might have guessed something of the sort had happened. That long silence without a word from or about his boy should have alerted him that something was wrong. Seán couldn't stop thinking of Father Martin's story. How his own father had cursed him to death at sea. By withholding his blessing and wishing sorrow on his efforts, had Seán condemned Callum to the same fate? A cold and frantic struggle all alone and doubting even his own father's love for him? And Seán knew now the strength and power of his own maledictions.

"This is my doing . . ." Seán said to Finn, who had made a nest on the old man's lap. "I'm to blame." Seán's mind was filled with fearsome images of his son alone in a small boat. He pictured him as he used to be, just a skinny little boy, clinging helplessly to a thwart before being ripped from it and sucked down, down by the terrible force of a whirlpool, bludgeoned, battered, and broken against the rocks. It made every bone in his body ache to think of it. Made his stomach ill with the imagining of his little boy's last moments. He gouged the heels of his hands into his watery eyes and groaned, "I can't bear it!"

Night fell upon Seán like a smothering cloak and his breathing grew more rapid and shallow until he felt he could not breathe at all and gasped, "What can I do?" He turned desperately to Muireann's chair, but it kept a solemn silence. "I thought I'd lost everything when I lost you, but it seems there's always something more to lose . . . it's nothing more than I deserve." His gasps made him dizzy, but he dared not close his eyes and risk replaying the dreadful imaginings of Callum's death at sea. He dared not sleep for fear he might visit the scene repeatedly in his dreams. He simply stared at Muireann's chair and clung to Finn.

Seán did not leave the cottage for three days after the letter. Would not leave his chair or let himself sleep. He held vigil and pondered and wept for shame. He would not see Father Martin even though the priest had continued to row out to Thréig each of those days to be with him. But Seán couldn't bear to see the young man's high stooping shoulders, like a fledgling falcon. Could not see his large, gentle hands, or springing boyish gait without pain. Only Finn brought him any comfort. Finn, whom he had never failed nor betrayed in any way. Finn, who asked for nothing but love. Though, after all, wasn't that all Callum had wanted? Wasn't that all anyone ever wanted?

Seán sat with his sorrows, his fears, and his uncertain future clinging to Finn until the evening of the third day when something deep inside him seemed to break loose. He felt it happen like an enormous wrench followed by a sense of absolute certainty. He stumbled from his chair and burst through the cottage door, like Jonah expelled from the belly of the great fish onto the shingle-shore a steaming, reeking wreck. Father Martin was sitting in the garden by Muireann's rose bush waiting and stood to meet him.

"I'm going anyway, Father. I'll make my own search for him, and though he's likely dead as they say, I'll still make my pilgrimage to Saint Columcille's island, and there I'll make what peace I can, one way or an- other." Seán marched to the sheep shed with Father Martin following si- lently behind. "It will take some time to mend it, but—" Seán faltered at the entrance to the shed, clutching at the door frame for support. Before him stood the currach, patched where the oar had smitten it, and a fresh coat of tar sealed it so the scar could scarcely be seen. A little bottle of holy water sat on the work bench with a prayer book.

"Shall we Christen her now? Before you leave?"

Seán was speechless with choking tears. All he could manage to croak out was, "You blessed boy! Oh, you blessed, blessed boy!"

That evening the currach was christened, invoking the prayers of both Saint Columcille and Saint Brendan the Navigator. She was given the name of *Corncrake* as seemed only fitting.

"I may not be back, you know."

"I know that Seán."

"You'll not try to stop me? Make me see sense?"

"If it were my fate to be lost at sea—alive, missing, and no longer looked for—what greater hope could I cling to but that my own father would come searching for me. I pray you find him."

"May I have your blessing for this voyage, Father?" Seán said, taking his cap in his hand.

Father Martin smiled and placed his right hand on Seán's bowed gray head. He closed his eyes and prayed, "O God, our heavenly Father, whose glory fills the whole of creation, and whose presence we find wherever we go: preserve your servant as he travels; surround him with your loving care; protect him from every danger; and bring him in safety to his journey's end . . ."

Seán replaced his cap and flung his arms around the young priest as though embracing his own son.

"Just bring me back a tear of Saint Columcille, won't you, Seán?"

"I don't know what that is, Father."

"You'll know it when you see it."

PART III

THE FISHERMAN, THE CAT, AND THE SEA

1

A PERSON STANDING ON THE shore at dawn might have seen it against the gray horizon, that single square sail, low slung, billowing out before the open boat, swept along by the spray and a capricious March wind. One might have seen the boat shudder with every wave that lapped its bow as it rose and dipped to the rhythm of the sea. Or might have noticed the bent silhouette of an elderly mariner, alone, minding both the ropes and the rudder in a clumsy, unpracticed way with a heavy dark hump on his shoulder. Was the man a hunchback? Did some dark fate weigh on him from behind, driving him out to sea? Or did some terrified land-loving creature cling to him as he sailed?

The wind had been fresh starting out in the still dark morning, which had meant a hard pull out from the cove in a boat much larger and heavier than he was used to, before Seán could finally raise the sheet. But when he did, the *Corncrake* leapt forward with a life all her own. With the cold wind stinging the leathery folds of his face and making his nose drip, Seán marveled at the strangeness of his circumstances. How was it that he, at his age, was setting out to sea like Saint Brendan in a sailing currach with a terrified cat digging its claws into his shoulders and back? It was not the heroic scene he had imagined as a child. If he was honest with himself, there were already misgivings bubbling up in the back of his mind—how nice a hot cup of tea by the fire might be, with Finn calmly sleeping on his lap. Much more comfortable than this cold, wet, and frankly painful start toward an uncertain destination, if in fact there *was* a destination. But there was no Muireann waiting for him back at home, and perhaps no Callum waiting out there to be found. There was only this isolated, uncertain moment.

Now that he was on his way, he felt like a tiny seed floating on a leaf, bearing within himself a certain, yet unknown fate. His leaf, the *Corncrake*, dipped and rose . . . dipped and rose in the heavy Atlantic swell. The sail

flapped, and Finn clung. That was the only reality now. He was no longer himself—or *himself* was no longer the same man, now that he'd left his island and set to sea, straining out against a current that seemed to tug him back toward all that he had ever known or been. Time itself seemed to withdraw like the tide when it leaves a chattering and a whispering in the sand, riddled with the bubbles and tunnels of secret, hidden things—protean forms caught in the midst of changing state. Now he too must wait in the space between past and future, to see what his own new shape might be.

Seán skirted the jagged coastline, indented with little exposed bays and jutting rocky headlands. He glanced back at Thréig only once as it receded from view in a blueish silver mist. The *Corncrake* handled well enough, though there was a knack to minding everything himself. He had planned on having an extra pair of hands, and Finn's clutching at him with needly claws was proving a hindrance. Still, as the morning broke, silent fulmars sliced the sky above the cliffs while he passed inside of Toraigh Island. Seán noticed them. Noticed their curved wings and their swooping flight. He was struck by their sudden and startling beauty as they skimmed the surface of the water, fishing for squid, jellyfish, and the like. His heart rose with them as they carried off the wriggling little translucences dangling from their beaks. He knew that this early in the spring they had not begun their breeding season yet and fished only for themselves that morning, but he imagined how a fine catch such as this would support the little cliff-dwelling families a few months later.

How odd, that you can see something every day of your life without really noticing it or appreciating its likeness to yourself. Callum would have known all the seabirds' names in Latin—what they ate and how they found it, how they nested, and where they spent their winters. The boy had often mentioned Toraigh Island for its seabirds, but mostly for its summer puffins and, of course, its colony of corncrakes. What was it the boy had said? Was it Toraigh he said that had the highest concentration of corncrakes in Ireland? So close, and yet Seán never took him there to see them. Had his boy been with him now, they could have stopped and stayed as long as Callum wanted. Seán turned away from the sight of Toraigh's noisy, white-streaked cliffs and sailed on.

He watched as Horn Head rose six hundred imposing feet out of the sea before him like a monster from one of Muireann's stories—*Fomhóraigh*, those fierce giants who rose up from under the sea. He clutched his chest, not for pain, but for beauty. She would have loved to see it. At that point,

Finn had cautiously crept down into the belly of the *Corncrake* and huddled in a lump between Seán's boots. His face was scrunched furiously as droplets of spray wet his fur and clung to his long whiskers.

They sailed close north from Sheep Haven to Lough Swilly, and by the time they passed the Fanad Head with its gleaming white lighthouse, the cat had fallen busily to grooming himself, shaking his paws in annoyance when the spray happened to re-wet him. Before long, Finn was creeping around the boat and peering with interest over the side at the frothy waves and watching the birds that swooped down from the cliffs.

"Perhaps you'll live up to your name after all, brave Fionn mac Cumhaill," Seán said as he rubbed the itching welts in this shoulder where Finn had hooked into him. He smiled at the cat's wide yellow eyes as it examined one new sight and smell after another before finally climbing into the bow. There he stood atop their bundles of supplies and ballast as grand and imposing as an old ship's figurehead.

The morning had been fair and the waypoints clearly visible so far as they sailed up the craggy coast, and Seán smiled as he remembered tracing the page from Father Martin's atlas, examining all the little havens, bays, and inlets which he now saw materializing before him. He knew what Father Martin would say if he could see these rugged cliffs and bays. As on that first morning on Thréig, when they began building the currach, the young priest would have exclaimed, making the sign of the cross, "Lord have mercy! Such a sight finds me quite unworthy!" Seán had laughed then because he was used to Thréig and its sunrises, at least as much as a man could be used to such sights. Now he felt the full force of what Father Martin had felt that morning and was intensely glad for the first time since Muireann's passing, that he was alive. But Seán could not linger on these feelings. His hip had at some point begun to ache, and his brow furrowed as he considered what that pain had come to mean in his last few years. He glanced up at the sky.

Clouds had begun to close in, and the atmosphere was rapidly thickening about him. It happened this way sometimes. So quickly the weather could turn, but this time there was no familiar shore and shelter to make for. Poor visibility could obscure his waymarks making it difficult to keep clear of the land and the many hazardous offshore islands and reefs that fronted it. Moreover, he knew there were no havens here into which a vessel, without specific local knowledge, could confidently enter in a gale.

Cautiously, and as quickly as he could make the *Corncrake* go, he made for Malin Head to find safe harbor before the storm should break loose.

Overhead the puffy white clouds were darkening and coming down nearly on top of him as the wind began to rise up in gusts. The *Corncrake* creaked and shuddered as a wave broke over her bow and drenched the furious Finn. Seán clenched his teeth and reached to lower the halyard as wisps of fog slithered past him and biting drops of cold rain and hail started spitting down at intervals. This coast was hazardous in fair weather to those who didn't know it well, but with the sky closing in around him, the headlands fading fast from view, and the wind beginning to howl in the rigging, Seán's heart began to sink with realization. He was sailing this open vessel into the face of a rising williwaw.

2

Seán tucked Finn, protesting, inside his raincoat as a mountainous wave rose up and the *Corncrake* tilted back. Time seemed to linger and nearly halt as she climbed, slowly, agonizingly as though she might never clear the top of it but might slip backwards into the fathomless depths below. Then came the deathly pause. She teetered on the brink with half the length of her hull jutting out over the face of the wave. Seán felt sick with fear that she might just snap in half like a twig—for such she was, after all: a bunch of twigs tied with string. Instead, the bottom dropped out of his stomach as Time leapt back into motion and the *Corncrake* plummeted along the foaming crest, flinging her pilot forward into her cavernous belly.

He clung to a thwart with one arm while holding hard to Finn, still tucked in his coat, with the other. A heartrending crack split the air as the lowered halyard swung, striking him on the side of the head. He squeezed shut his eyes against the pain and against the stinging spray, then his mind itself tilted and slipped . . . it spun as though being sucked through a funnel into dark, interstellar space, with shapeless blurs and dazzles leaping, coalescing, and receding like comets in the void. He was no longer *here* and *now* in the belly of the pitching *Corncrake*. He was *no*where. He was *every*where. And then, finally, he was *other*where—*there* . . . on the rock. *His* rock, in *his* cove.

He sat there dripping, wrapped in heavy rain gear, watching a small ship on the distant horizon. It was tossed about on the waves like a toy boat in a child's bath. He pitied the foolish mariner who tried to sail such a vessel along this perilous coast in such a violent squall as this. It seemed as though all of the storm's fury was concentrated on that one weak boat—on that one weak man. Seán watched, breathless, paralyzed on the rock in his own cove, as the little boat teetered suspended at the top of each wave before plummeting down the foamy slopes of sea.

With each dive, he expected the boat to be broken up into kindling, but again and again it rose up to the summits and plunged down into the watery canyons. In the midst of the jagged range of snow-capped waves, a hill of shining, slippery flesh began to rise above the surface, followed by another, and another. They rose in rolling black loops from the endragoned upboiling of the sea, surrounding the boat. The *Oilliphést*? Here? In this fishless desert? Feeding on the only prey left: the last of the small-boat fishermen? Seán wanted to scream aloud, but he had no voice. He wanted to leap up from the rock, but he had no strength in his body to move. That ship—that man—would surely meet death in the gullet of the ancient sea-snake!

Hot salty tears slithered down his cold cheeks. "Lord have mercy. . ." he heard himself whispering repeatedly in his mind's ear. "Lord have mercy . . ." The loops of shining flesh encircled the little currach, streaming salty foam and weeds as the head of the beast itself rose high in the air above the boat with sharp-toothed jaws wide open as if ready to strike. "Lord have mercy . . ."

Suddenly the air grew murmurous with whispers. Not the harsh crashing that is the sea's voice in a gale, mingling with the noise of his own mind, but the roar like a mighty wind made up of many voices whispering at once. Language, but not words—aching and throbbing with meaning and urgency above the tumult of the storm.

Seán slid his eyes sideways, for they alone of all his parts would move. Beyond the furthest corner of his vision, somewhere behind his head, where no one ought to be able to see anything at all, he saw them. He saw them and he knew who they were, though they were none of them in their right forms. He knew who they were because they could be no one else. The dove flickered like white flame and seemed to call lightning down crackling from the black sky. The other bird, like a huge voyaging albatross joined the wordless whispering as it hovered on powerful sail-like wings. A shadowy woman, a mere wisp of a girl, with hair flowing out from her like seaweed threw herself from the cliff into the water, swimming like a salmon in the waves. A thin man who seemed either very old or very young, with high, hunched shoulders spread wide his arms which grew also into wings and pitched himself off the cliff like a falcon hurtling towards its prey. The wind roared with all their combined whispers and the sky flashed with the dove's lightning.

The *Oilliphést*, seizing its chance, struck with gaping blood-red maw and swallowed the ship whole in spite of the birds diving at its face, pecking at its eyes and ripping its flesh with sharp talons. The salmon-woman flung herself through the waves at the creature brandishing in her hand a gleaming white shell, its edge sharp as a knife's blade. She threw herself upon the writhing sea serpent and slit it open from belly to jaws, hauling the hapless fisherman from his tomb and dragging him through the turbulent waters towards the shore. Then a roar that was neither the gale nor the dying monster, split the air and throbbed like thunder behind Seán's eyes. All was dark. The birds, the mermaid, the monster, and the sea all retreated into the dark, and silence enveloped Seán like thick, black wool.

He swam through the shapeless murk, every muscle in his arms screaming until out of that darkness he squeezed himself—out of that black woolen silence and into the light of the familiar shore where all memory made its home. *Am I dead or dreaming…* he wondered as he looked around him at the calm sea. He found himself swept along like a cloud without legs, without effort or will, around the corner of his mind and slipping into a day long ago. He knew the day at once by the strained gray sky that rendered everything else nearly colorless as well. He remembered the vantage point, the view, and panic that tasted like death.

Had *he* been so reckless at that age? Seán could hardly remember being six. Snatches here and there of mother, father, fire, and food. Did he ever throw down his boots and climb barefooted up the cliff face? He remembered the feel of cold, wet granite—the rough grain and texture—the red, sanded fingertips and toes, aching with cold—scraping the entire front of himself raw sliding down after a misstep. He must have done it too, but it had been gut-wrenching to watch as a father. That downy head, ruffled in the sea breeze, inching higher and higher up the cliff. Too high. One slip at that height would mean death on the rocks below. Did he dare even to shout the boy's name and risk distracting him from his grips and footholds?

Callum had never been one to seek out danger, but often enough it had found him. He must have wanted something badly to take his little life in his own hands and scale the cliff. Seán had stood paralyzed watching. He didn't dare call to Muireann. He was meant to be minding the child while she rested, but he'd been distracted in bating lobster creels, and had gone on talking to a boy who had long since wandered off. Should he climb up after him? Would there be any use? If the boy froze and took fright, would

he be able to do anything for him at all? Seán watched, transfixed, his ears ringing. . . good lord . . . the boy had stopped climbing.

He was stuck; Seán was sure of it. He couldn't find his next grip and would soon panic and fall. The seconds expanded infinitely, and the screaming seabirds swooped and dove around the little figure, so high up the cliff. But the boy clung, stuck hard like a barnacle, peering into a rock crevice. Seán groaned as one of the little hands let go of its grip and reached into the crevice to touch something too small to be seen from the ground. The boy hung there one-handed examining whatever it was, seemingly unaware of his proximity to death. Finally, the loose hand found a new grip and the skinny little figure started inching upward once more.

Seán released the breath he'd been holding. He watched—watched the boy make his way finally to the top of the cliff and stand too near the edge looking down from whence he'd come, before turning to skip home. Relief washed over Seán like a wave, but anger had followed close on its heels.

"What were you thinking, Callum! You could've fallen! You could've died!" Seán blasted the boy in the garden that evening, grabbing him by his skinny little wing, torn between the desire to embrace him and cuff him. "C'mere to me, child! I'll brain ya!" The desire to embrace won out and he fairly crushed the boy to his chest. "What did you think you were you doing all the way up there?"

The boy scrunched his bare toes in the grass and avoided his father's eyes.

"Well?"

"There's chicks," he whispered.

"There's what?"

"Chicks. The Kittiwakes have chicks. They're so soft, Daddy . . . they're up there in the crags in little mud and seaweed nests, just tucked away and waiting for their supper . . . they're so soft . . ." *But you're soft!* Seán had wanted to say. *You're so soft! And soft things are so easily broken . . .* But he had just stood there, still holding that skinny little arm that offered no resistance. Seán had felt old and ill, even then—as precarious as the boy on the cliff had been. How easy it would be to lose everything.

"Those chicks will grow feathers and fly one day. But this wee thing. . ." he said, flapping the weak little arm, "you could have fallen and died today, and you aren't allowed! You aren't allowed to die before me!"

The little boy smiled, for children don't fear death as grownups do.

"Then Saint Columcille would come and fly away with me to the back of the North Wind."

"And what would *I* do then? Without my own chick!"

The boy looked at him sideways through one eye, then the other. His mouth opened as though to speak but shut again with a clack. The skinny little wing in Seán's hand had sprouted rows of long mottled brown feathers, and with a rustle, the boy took flight.

* * *

It was a rough, rasping tongue flickering under his earlobe that brought Seán into the daylight. His shuttered lids pealed back to a confused rush of sideways thoughts. His eyes ached as though they'd been put in wrong. He was not in his cove or in his chair, or anywhere he ought to be. The sky was woolen gray above him, and Finn's scrunched face was glaring at him. The cat's soggy body looked barely half its proper size, and his eyes were blackened wide with terror. Seán took hold of the cat and crushed its furious face to his chest in relief.

"You're alive!" his voice quavered through the ringing in his ears. "And so am I . . . I think." He craned his aching neck to peer over the gunwale and get a look around. They were wrapped in a thick blanket of fog that obscured his view in all directions, but there was no motion of the sea. It was as if they were pinned in place atop a wave, wrapped in unnatural calm.

"How long was I out?" he asked the cat, who simply pressed into Seán's body for warmth and sneezed into his dripping raincoat. Seán rocked gently in place to feel how stable their situation was. The *Corncrake* creaked and scraped under them, then a ripping noise drew his eyes to a sharp point of granite, like a fang, jutting through the middle of the boat. They were pinned in place after all on some sharp outcropping. Water was seeping into the bottom of the boat around the puncture site. Cold drops fell on his head from the sail, torn and lank, hanging like a white flag of defeat.

Seán reached clumsy, blueish fingers down into the boat to find an oar. He extended it as far into the mist as he could. It scraped against a wall of rock to the starboard—a cliff, maybe. He feared the boat would take on too much water if he waited for the fog to lift, and it might not blow clear for some time. More rain could blast down again—the sky was that low, steely hardness that could throw down anything at any moment. He tried crawling toward his packs in the bow to fetch supplies for patching the rend, but

the boat started to tilt like a scale with his shifting weight, and the fang of granite dug deeper into the *Corncrake's* belly.

Seán sat weighing his options, cringing as he rubbed a hot painful swelling at the place where the halyard had struck his temple. He stopped, groping frantically at his left breast pocket. It was still safe. He pressed Muireann's Easter glove to his cheek in relief. As he did so, a kittiwake hovered low above him, spectral in the fog, like a white sheet of paper caught on a breeze. She landed atop the mast and looked down at him through shining black eyes, calling out shrilly, as though to offer her own advice. Oddly, he felt as if he understood her as clearly as if she'd spoken to him in human speech. He nodded in agreement. All possible courses of action seemed to dwindle down into one least doomed. He must leave everything behind—everything but Finn—and climb.

3

S EÁN LEFT HIS BOOTS behind. He would need to feel the rock beneath his feet to be sure of his footholds. He strapped Finn to his back with some bits of rope and torn canvas from the sail. Furry legs and splayed toes hung out behind him so that the cat couldn't dig his claws into Seán's back as he climbed. The fog was still so dense that he couldn't yet see the top of the cliff or how long and hard this climb was bound to be. But the *Corncrake* was filling with cold seawater, and he couldn't reach any of his supplies without dislodging her. He reached out to the nearest outcropping and stepped cautiously out of the boat.

Seán hummed to calm his nerves. Songs he'd heard as a child, or those sung by the traveling fiddler in the pub, half remembered but which fixed him as much to reality as to the cliff. He hummed the songs of the old heroes that his mermaid used to sing by the fireside in foul weather to entertain their little boy. *Well, Muireann,* he thought. *I'm old and I'm roving about. Is this what you meant? I can't see above me or below me. I can only see my next grip as I come to it . . . and trust that there will be one at all.* Finn yowled hoarse and miserable as they crept slowly up the slippery, white-streaked rock face amid the eerie warning screams of the rupestral colony nesting there. The sharp odor of ammonia scoured his nasal passages like steel wool and made his eyes water. But every reach found a hand hold, however smeared with layers of guano, and up he hauled himself. As Seán slid his hand into a crevice to steady his next upward push he felt something so soft it could barely be felt at all by his cold, calloused fingers. He peered in to see two wobbling white downy heads. Four shiny round eyes peered back at him expectantly.

"Oh! Sorry to disturb you! My, but you are soft, aren't you! I'm sure your Mammy will be back soon—don't fuss."

Seeing those dark, shining eyes in the rock, thinking of the boy who risked his neck just to see and touch their like all those years ago, Seán smiled. His face was stiff with cold, but his own climb seemed somehow pre-ordained as these fresh gusts of memory swept over him. He hadn't understood it then. He had been too wrinkled and calloused of heart. How sad to think that only now—now that he was wrinkled and calloused of body—his heart might be growing young again. He climbed on.

He climbed through the swooping, whooping, and warning of the nesting seabirds who beat against him valiantly with gusting wings and sharp beaks when he came too near their nests. He climbed through the screams, aches, and spasms of his own muscles as they strained against his own weight and Finn's. He climbed through the thick white uncertainty of the fog, until he started to doubt whether any of this really was happening to him at all.

Perhaps it was all just another dream, or some other such dysfunction of reality. At some point soon a rough barbed tongue might scour his earlobe and his eyes would drag open to the dying peat fire and blue dawn in his chair. Perhaps if he just let go of his grip on the rock, he would fall to waking as he had so many times before. That was one way to end this unpleasant dream, but he didn't dare risk it, perchance he really was perched on some unknown cliff with a cat on his back, absurd as it all seemed. Anyway, he was cold, wet, and all of his red-sanded fingers and toes were sore. His whole face ached with the cold and with the pungent odor of seabird guano and decaying seaweed. Those details felt all too real, and he must climb either until he ran out of strength and fell to his death or reached the top of whatever land this was.

Seán tried to estimate how far he'd climbed, but fog clung to the cliff almost as desperately as he did. He could either be several boat lengths above the *Corncrake*, or mere inches. Just as his soul was sinking into despair and his shaking arms were freezing up, he felt grass under his fingers, and heaved himself onto either the summit, or some grassy shelf.

Seán lay on his stomach in the wet grass gasping for breath and shaking with cold and exertion. Here he determined to rest in the snowy drifts of fog until he could see better where he'd landed. Finn had gone quiet, perhaps with relief. Seán reached around weakly to loosen the ropes and let the cat out of the sling. Finn shook himself and huddled close, leaning into Seán's pounding chest. The cat's warmth soothed his trembling, and he closed his eyes to the teeming emptiness of the fog.

* * *

The dream seemed to reach him like light from a star—old light—the source of which was long gone. Seán dreamed himself in his old chair by the fire, a woolen blanket wrapped around him and a hot baked potato in each hand. The warmth was beautiful on his cold, aching fingers. He sensed the familiar rumble of Finn's purring on his lap and felt himself safe. He sat, a silent spectator to past scenes: himself as a younger man seated on the floor by the fire with a tiny Callum, no older than four or five, sorting through a box of pebbles, shells, bones, and feathers. But it wasn't a dream of what *had* been, after all. Not like the usual kind that brought back his most comfortable memories. For he had never sat with Callum like that, listening to incoherent babbling about his collections. Callum had hidden his treasures away like something too good to be seen. They had most often sat in silence while Muireann sang or read aloud to them.

In this dream they spread out the smooth, wave-polished pebbles, cowries, and speckled feathers on the floor and sorted through them admiringly, talking and talking. They were both incoherent—the specters both of child and father. Both talked and talked yet never seemed to say anything, at least nothing that held any meaning to Seán. It was this way perhaps because it was only a vision of what could, or *should* have been, never brought to life through real speech and action.

Seán's eyes were dim and foggy as he watched the dream of the man and his little boy by the fire, their backs to him in his chair. A tear trickled down his cheek and it felt real. Things that might have been have no words of their own, but regret is eloquent. Suddenly, a warm, soft hand rested on his shoulder and a woman's face, still misty to his eyes, bent near his own and spoke in that same incoherent dream-speech. His mind creaked with the effort to understand her words.

"Muireann . . ." he murmured to the blurred apparition kneeling beside him. The dream-Muireann spoke again to him, and the dream-speech changed in tone, shifted, and seemed to tune itself. The words began sliding into meaning even as fiddle strings slide finally into tune with the turn of a peg.

"Are you hurt?" she asked him. "Where have you come from?"

"I'm exploring, my darling. Just as you said I should," Seán said weakly. The whole of his mouth seemed numb, coated in salt and leftover fear. The incoherent dream-speech returned as the man turned from the boy on the

floor and spoke to the dream-Muireann. Both of them now knelt staring blurrily and, Seán thought, a little sadly into his face.

"Where did you start from?" dream-Muireann asked him.

"The end, my darling. The end is where I started from," Seán said with a pang, for the truest words often stung him now that way. He wondered why these misty dream figures concerned themselves with questions they must already know the answers to, in the usual way of dream specters. The two figures fell to whispering and the dream-Muireann stood up to fetch something. She returned shortly with a glass which she held to his lips, with one warm hand placed gently behind his head. Seán sucked from the glass's rim a smoky amber liquid. It burned his lips and tongue and tasted of a peat fire, though it was cool. It burned as it traveled down his throat and into his stomach. Finally, it burned even the fog from his vision. The worried faces of the specters came into focus before his eyes, and he did not know them.

"Where am I?"

4

ANGUS AND BRIGID WERE hard to understand unless they talked especially slow and distinct for him. Seán had never traveled outside of
County Donegal and their accents puzzled him. Diarmad was worst of all,
for he had a toddler's lisp and tendency toward halting monotone. Thank-
fully, few words were required between any of them as Brigid tenderly led
Seán to Diarmad's bed and piled him with woolen blankets and hot water
bottles. She shut the door saying very slowly, and a little louder than necessary, that he was to rest.

Seán, in his weakness, couldn't refuse Brigid's maternal care and found
himself deeply grateful in spite of his confusion, or perhaps because of it.
He gathered that Angus had discovered him near the shore—though that
hadn't made sense, after his perilous climb up the cliff. They must have a
different word for cliff or something in their strange dialect. The younger
man must be incredibly strong to have hauled him back to their cottage in
his heavy wet gear, and he could only assume Finn had followed. Or had
he? Where was the cat now? He tried to raise his head and look about for
him, but at that moment Brigid came in with a mug of tea and something
she called tatty scones, which he would have called potato cakes, or very
like.

"No, no, no . . ." she scolded, shaking her head in the same slow exag-
gerated way that she spoke to him. "Rest! Eat!"

"My cat?" Seán said and made a meowing sound in case it was as hard
for her to understand him as it was for him to understand her.

"With Diarmad. The wee boy. Don't worry." She eased him back onto
the pillow and tucked him in like a child.

With Diarmad. So, Finn had made it with him to this little safe haven.
Good. Seán let Brigid plump the pillow to support his neck before sitting
in a chair by the bed holding a tatty scone before his lips with one hand

held underneath his chin to catch the crumbs. He was familiar with this practical gesture and had used it himself with Muireann. How strange to be cared for. Seán felt his cheeks beginning to burn. He felt torn between feelings of gratitude and embarrassment. He smiled apologetically up at Brigid in that slightly perturbed way one does when receiving help one wishes one didn't need in the first place. This brought back memories of the many times Muireann had apologized to him in similar circumstances.

"I'm sorry, Love," she'd say as he bathed her with a sponge or tended her bedpan. "I'm so sorry." He had been annoyed by her apologies then. It wasn't as if she'd taken ill on purpose to make extra work for him to do. He didn't resent caring for her. He never did. He ached for her pain, wept for her frustration at her own diminishing capabilities, but never had he resented caring for her. It was something he could give her when she was losing everything. Now he understood how his care had pierced her with guilt. The guilt of a caretaker who can no longer care for oneself. The guilt of feeling like a burden. The guilt of feeling somehow responsible for one's fragility. He understood her apologies now—understood them and wept.

"Do you have pain?" Brigid asked very slowly, enunciating each word clearly, but strangely.

"None that tears can't cure," he said, laying his old, cold claw of a hand on her smooth one. "Thank you for your kindness." He smiled up at her again but did not apologize.

Seán drifted into a dreamless sleep that seemed just an instant but must have been hours. He woke to the sound of rather juicy mouth-breathing and opened his eyes to a plump pink face hovering next to his own, staring. A huge moist smile spread across it as Seán blinked it into focus.

"Look!" Diarmad held out a handful of varied pebbles, worn smooth by the tide, and poured them in a little heap on Seán's chest. Seán squinted down at them and sorted through the little pile with a gnarled forefinger. He lingered over their colors, shapes, and textures before looking into the little boy's face, seeing momentarily his own Callum looking out from those smiling eyes.

"They're beautiful."

*　*　*

After a few days of rest under Brigid's strict supervision, and after examining the majority of Diarmad's extensive rock collection while his mother

was busy with her own work in the kitchen garden, Seán's strength began to return. One morning early he woke and dressed in his own clothes that Brigid had washed, mended, and draped over the back of a chair for him. He emerged to find Finn chasing and pouncing on a piece of string that Diarmad dragged across the floor. Angus rose from his chair smiling and lordly.

"You're better, then?"

"Yes. . .er, my boat?" Seán asked slowly.

"Oh, right, right. Come with me. You too, Diarmad. Wellies." The little boy ran to pull on a pair of rubber rain boots and a jacket that was several sizes too big for him. "It's not going anywhere soon, so I left it till you were fit."

The three of them hiked out across a barren boggy stretch of earth that squelched and sucked with each step. Seán looked all around him, seeing for the first time the lay of the land he'd found. Two large, rounded humps rose out of the ground—mountains topped in fog and surrounded in slippery shale.

"Paps of Jura," Angus said tilting his head toward them.

"Jura?"

"Jura . . . that's where we are."

Seán stared at him in amazement. How was it possible that the storm had blown him so close to the place he needed to be?

"Where is it you're trying to get to?" Angus asked.

"Well, here actually . . . and Scarba. Iona eventually."

"Ah. A pilgrim, are you?"

"Something like that."

They continued to hike a short way until Angus stopped and indicated the spot where he'd discovered Seán. But this couldn't be right. Where was the massive cliff he'd scaled? There was only a little rocky drop to the shore, a few boat lengths at most. He walked to the edge and looked down. Sure enough, there was the Corncrake, stuck on a rock, half-filled with seawater. He blushed, shaking his head.

"The fog played tricks on me, I suppose."

"It'll do that. You're not the first, nor will you be the last. Lucky I found you, though, when I did. You were stone cold and unconscious, only the wee cat giving you warmth. Probably saved you."

"Finn," Seán nodded. "I saved him as an orphan; it seems he returned me the favor." Seán looked forlornly down at the wounded currach.

127

"It looks an easy enough fix, you know. Shall we bring her up?" Angus slipped a coil of thick rope off his shoulder and didn't wait for an answer before climbing down toward the sharp boulders fronting the headland. It was low tide and the area around the rock that held the *Corncrake* was shallow and weedy. Angus fixed the rope to one end and tossed the length up to Seán. By degrees, through Seán's pulling and Angus's pushing and jiggling, they freed the *Corncrake* from the granite tooth and hauled her up to dry land. Diarmad jumped up and down clapping his chubby, dimpled hands.

As they carried the *Corncrake* back toward the cottage, Seán began to notice little roped off areas of land around the cottage that didn't look like typical garden plots. Some had insects swarming above heaps of decomposing seaweed spread across the barren ground. Seán gestured questioningly toward it.

"That? An experiment," Angus responded with a rakish smile and a wink. *Experiment.* Seán began to wonder if Angus was a crofter at all . . . but what else would he be doing on this barren and sparsely populated little island?

5

ERHAPS SEÁN HAD BEEN in a hurry. He'd never been one for sitting still or resting long. His will had returned, and he mistook it for strength. Hauling up the boat had done something. He noticed the twinge and ignored it—pushed through it. Then, as they carried the *Corncrake* back to Brigid and Angus's cottage, the twinge came alive and distinct and other from him. He'd never felt anything quite like it in his life. As he bent to set down the end he was carrying and moved to straighten back up again, the muscles in his lower back caught as if on a great barbed fishhook. They hardened, squeezed, and changed shape with an angry will of their own. He stumbled down to his hands and knees, digging his fingers into the mud and groaning with pain. Brigid ran from the kitchen garden scolding Angus.

"Too soon! He wasn't fully recovered! Why did you let him haul up that boat?"

"He asked to go and fetch it," Angus said with a helpless shrug.

"He should have been at least one more day resting! Now look! He's worse off than before! Bring him in gently, Angus. Gently!"

Diarmad's plump pink face puckered, and he began to cry, seeing the old man writhing in pain.

"Diarmad, go play now. Mummy'll get it sorted."

Seán was only vaguely aware of Angus and Brigid supporting him, laying him back in Diarmad's bed. Brigid was talking fast and giving orders, pulling off Seán's boots and fetching a hot water bottle wrapped in a flannel. For the next twenty-four hours, she nursed him. She hardly left his side and talked constantly, like a soul who has had precious little opportunity of talking for far too long. She talked of this and that, of her garden and her child, but mostly of muscles and their names and what they did when they were angry. Seán lay still and listened to her. Eventually he became so

accustomed to her talking that the strange accent which had confounded him when he arrived started to sound almost normal to his ear.

Under Brigid's dedicated care, the muscles in Seán's back began to loosen. Then, she gave him strict instructions about feeble little stretches that he resented, but obediently performed. Seán didn't dare say *no* to Brigid.

"How do you know all of these things, my darling? About different muscles and how to fix a bad back and all?"

"I was a nurse before, at a hospital in Edinburgh. That's where I met Angus. Poor darling was having his tonsils out and I was on duty. He could barely even speak, but he still managed to ask me out with him." She smiled, gazing at the memory as though it were somewhere in the distance, still happening.

"You're not from Jura, then?" Seán asked.

"No, no. I'm a city girl, but I'm learning. We've been here about a year now."

"Why? Why Jura of all places?" Seán asked as he gripped his knee with fingers interlaced, pulling it gently toward his chest in a long, slow stretch.

"Well, it's not too remote, but not too many people either—mostly barren. It's perfect, really."

Seán looked at her incredulously.

"Well . . . I mean it's perfect for the kind of research Angus wants to do. He's an ecologist, you know."

"I didn't know. Is that why he has those roped-off areas? With the seaweed?"

"Yes, that's part of his research. He's looking for ways to improve the soil quality in deforested areas of the highlands and islands." Brigid gazed out the window from her chair by the bed, watching Angus with his notebook, poking around the rotting seaweed, taking samples in little glass tubes, and jotting down notes with a pencil that he kept tucked behind one ear.

"Are you not lonely out here? After the big city, I mean," Seán asked.

She gave him a resolute smile, involving her lips, but not quite her eyes.

"Ach no. It's the way life ought to be, isn't it? At one with nature—and nature needs us now, doesn't it? It's people that injured it, and people that have to heal it. It's not an easy life we've got out here, but Angus's work is

important . . . *quite* important. We both believe in it. Are you from a larger town yourself, Seán? You never mentioned where you started from."

"No, no. I'm an islander myself, from birth."

"Are you indeed? What island is that?"

"You won't know it. I was the last to leave it and now it's just another isle of ruins that Time will soon forget. An isle of ghosts and birds and bog cotton. Thréig, it's called, and rightly so. It bore its end in its beginning, too. A *foresaken* place."

Brigid turned away from the window and examined Seán's face with sudden interest. A genuine smile began to spread across her face, which was then as quickly replaced with a look of deep sorrow.

"I'm so sorry, Seán," she said, finding her voice at last.

"Sorry? Why?"

"You're here—that means she really has died. I'm most awfully sorry for your loss."

"How do you . . .?" Seán stared at Brigid in disbelief.

"You'll be Callum's father, am I right?"

"You know my Callum?"

"Oh yes. He came to us the same as you—only quite a bit worse off. Caught up in the strait of Corryvrecken betwixt us and Scarba a few months back. We found him on the shore, barely alive."

Seán gripped the side of the bed and barely breathed for excitement.

"He was lucky, was your Callum. Lucky to wash up on an island with a nurse living on it." She winked at him.

"He's alive? My Callum's alive?" Seán gasped, tears welling up in his eyes. Brigid knelt down by the bed, placed her hand on his and squeezed it.

"Yes! Yes, Seán! Callum is alive! Did you not know?"

"I had a letter. They said he was missing and probably dead . . ."

"Irresponsible," she spat, angrily. "Nobody ever asked *us* if we'd seen him. Whoever *they* are they can't have looked very hard for him."

"Is he well? Where is he now?"

"You're looking for him, aren't you? You're making your own search and that's why you've come here, isn't it?"

"Where is my boy now?"

Brigid's eyebrows knit together in a little crease as she sighed.

"I couldn't tell you exactly, Seán. He was with us for several weeks as he healed. He had broken ribs and leg . . . countless abrasions. He could easily have died of infection if not exposure, but for my kit of supplies here

and ability to set a bone." She shuddered a little at that and swallowed. "He was in bed a long time. Ach, Diarmad *loved* him! He would sit by Callum for hours on end, right here in this very chair, showing him all his wee bits and pieces from the shore. And your Callum would listen and listen and tell him things. You raised a kind, gentle man, Seán. Patient. He's so like you!"

"No . . . no, he's not like me. His mother made him better than I ever was."

Brigid's face fell again.

"One night, Callum was terribly upset. He said he had the most dreadful feeling all of a sudden—cold and empty as an old bottle on the beach. He said he felt a rend in his heart like nothing he could describe. He said he was certain his mother had passed away."

Seán stared at Brigid in disbelief.

"He wept. I've never seen a young man weep so. Diarmad wept to see Callum weep, and I wept to see the two of them, and Angus wept to see me weep. It's a wonder we didn't all drown in the tears shed that night. He felt like family to us at that point, you see? Like family, and when your family hurts, you hurt with them. We hurt too, because we knew he would be leaving us soon. His bones were just about healed then, so he repaired his wee boat, and he left."

"When? Where did he go?" Seán's voice trembled.

"It was just last week. I can only say I thought he was planning to get back to the mainland and straight away charter a boat to Donegal. His was just a little rowing scull—you know, he was stationed at Mull and only rowed out short distances to camp a few days at a time on the smaller islands . . . for the birds, you know."

"But he should have gotten home before I left!"

"I don't know, Seán. I don't know where he could be or how you missed each other. I'm sorry I can't tell you more."

* * *

As Seán began to regain his strength and flexibility, he propped himself up with a pillow to see out the little window. He had been eager to leave before, but now that he knew Callum was out there to be found, he felt such an urgency to get out of that bed and into his boat he could hardly contain himself. The *Corncrake* lay on its gunwales where they'd left it when his back gave out, his supplies sheltering underneath it. In his mind, he

planned his repairs as he pulled his knees alternately to his chest, just as Brigid had instructed him. He lay back again and watched out the window, Brigid toiling in the kitchen garden, while Angus walked around with his notebook, visiting the experimental fields, turning the rotting seaweed with a pitchfork, and jotting down notes..

Diarmad seemed a law unto himself, going where he pleased and doing what he pleased while his parents worked. Seán watched the little boy with amusement as he hopped around like a rabbit, pretending that to land on a shadow meant instant death. He had watched the little boy die dramatically five or six times before he finally tired of his game and sat staring at a smooth white stone that he turned over and over in his hand.

Lonely, Seán thought. A lonely child. Happy when he had a game to play, or a job to do, but the look of blank anguish on the little boy's face when he sat there alone with his rock filled Seán with memories of his own island childhood, taken from school so young and put to work at his trade before his voice had even gone deep. Perhaps Callum had felt that loneliness as well, though Callum had been allowed to stay in school and had known at least a few other children, though he'd never shown as much interest in other children as he did in the birds.

Seán watched Diarmad's face from the window, so young and so suddenly sad. How easily a small body could be overlooked, and its feelings go unnoticed. He longed to be a little boy again, to make friends with Diarmad and to play chase. His back began to ache again, and he sighed. Seán imagined that only a few weeks ago, his own Callum would have been out there with little Diarmad, playing games with him and laughing. Now Diarmad sat like a little stone himself, waiting. What was he waiting for? The little boy's head rose slowly, and his eyes fixed on something with sudden interest. What was he looking at? Seán held his breath.

Diarmad's body was still, rigid, and restrained. He stared at something lurking around the foundations of the cottage. The boy blinked, and blinked again, slowly and with intention. He reached out a chubby hand and Finn came creeping out of the shadows. He smelled the outstretched hand, then bumped his head against it. A smile spread across Diarmad's round face as the cat leaned into his caresses. Seán smiled too and settled back into the pillows. *Good cat, Finn,* he sighed inwardly. *Good cat.*

Seán closed his eyes and thought through each repair he must make to the *Corncrake*, avoiding, for the moment, the one question that loomed above all others. Once the currach was ready to set sail again, where was he

to go? Ought he to simply make his way back to Thréig and wait for Callum to make his way there as well? If Thréig had been where Callum was heading straight away, he could have been there days before Seán had left. No, Callum had gone someplace else first, and as sleep engulfed him, bearing him on waves of dream toward gradually rising headlands of pre-conscious certainties, Seán suddenly knew where Callum must be.

6

When Seán awoke from his light, drifting sleep, Diarmad was sitting on the chair next to him, staring. The boy grinned to see the old man's eyes focus on him.

"You're Callum's papa," he said, and slid off the chair to the floor. He flung his plump arms around Seán and hugged him, smelling of biscuits and little boy. "I love Callum. He gave me a corncrake feather for my collection and drew me pictures of birds. Can you draw pictures, too?"

Seán smiled. Of course the boy loved Callum—Callum was one of those rare children who had managed to survive into adulthood without losing himself, and the boy had sensed their kinship. Children know other children, even the grown-up ones, just as birds know their own kind.

"I *am* Callum's papa, but Callum is better at drawing pictures than I am. I can build boats, though. Would you like to help me mend mine when I'm better?"

Diarmad's eyes widened, and he bounced up and down while still hugging Seán, which made his back threaten to twinge.

"Yes, yes, yes, yes! I'm a good helper! I want to help! Give me a job, *please*! Can you give me one right *now*?"

"Yes, Diarmad. I have a very important job for you to do. It will be hard, though. Do you think you can do a *hard* job?"

"Yes, I can," Diarmad said gravely with his plump little hand on his heart as though swearing a solemn oath.

"My poor cat, Finn, has had a terrible time. He saved me, you know, but I fear he needs some special care, himself. He's not used to being here yet and he needs a friend to help him feel happy while I recover my strength. He was very frightened in the storm that brought us here. It's hard to know what a cat is thinking. They don't speak our language, do they?"

"They say *meeeee-oooow*."

"Yes, that's right. Now, this is my job for you. Can you try some different ways to make him happy? Check if he's hungry. He likes little fishes and pieces of meat. He even likes breadcrumbs! See if he'd like to play games with you. See if he'd like to be held and stroked and talked to. He dearly loves to be told stories and scratched under his chin."

"But how will I know when he's happy?"

"Well, instead of saying *meow* he'll say *purrrrrr* like there are bunches of smooth stones tumbling and rumbling round in his chest. And his eyes will go narrow and very yellow. He'll let you know when you've made him happy. I know it's a hard job. Do you think you can you do it, Diarmad?"

"I *can* do it! I'll go and do it now!" And the little boy ran out of the room calling and searching for the cat. Seán twisted his torso a little to test out his back, and again performed his stretches. Soon. Very soon.

* * *

The next day, Seán began taking slow walks around the garden with Diarmad while Brigid and Angus worked. The slow walks began to increase in speed and scope as Seán became more limber. Diarmad jumped up and down waving his dimpled hands like little pink starfish when Seán said he was ready to get to work on the *Corncrake*. Angus came to join in the repairs as well, to Diarmad's acute disappointment.

"No, papa! *I'm* Seán's helper! He asked *me*!"

"I don't want you touching that tar, Diarmad. Your mother will murder me if you come back inside all black and stinky with that stuff."

Diarmad's face puckered up red and infinitely tragic as he sunk to the ground with his face in his hands, wailing silently.

"Oh, I've plenty of other good jobs for *you*, Diarmad," Seán said. "The tar really is nasty stuff. *I* don't even like to touch it myself. I might have your papa brush it on for me, so's I don't get all stinky neither."

The little boy staggered to his feet and wiped the tears from his face.

"Now this is a very important and careful job I have for you, Diarmad." Seán had the little boy hold the canvas patch in place while he stitched around it. "Do you know, I never taught my Callum how to build a currach, but I surely wish I had. It's grand having a great big boy to help me."

Diarmad cast a glance over his shoulder at Angus and grinned.

"See, papa! *I* do important work, too!"

Angus stroked his chin and smiled.

"So you do. Maybe I should give you jobs to do for me sometimes."

"Yes, yes, yes, *please!*"

"Don't jump now! Hold it still or I might just stab one of us with the awl!" Seán laughed as the little boy froze like a statue, unblinking and trying hard not to smile. "You're a good lad, Diarmad." Seán smiled back at Angus, who was looking at his little boy with wistful pride.

"He *is* a good lad. And daily growing."

The repairs were quickly finished with the help of so many hands. As the tar dried, Seán helped Diarmad build a toy boat from twisted reeds they collected.

"This wee boat won't need near so many knots as mine did to hold it together," Seán said as he guided Diarmad's slow fingers in binding the reeds with string. "Shall we make it a skin from this scrap of canvas?"

Diarmad nodded gravely, and they stretched the bit of extra canvas over the little frame, stitching it into place before dipping it in the remaining tar and letting it dry while they trimmed a little reed mast and fitted it with a square sail.

"What shall we call our wee ship?"

"The *Corncrake's Chick!*" Diarmad shouted without hesitation, and they floated it in a calm tide pool for its maiden voyage.

When the *Corncrake* herself was finally ready, and Seán was fit enough to sail, Brigid insisted on serving them up a fine feast to see him off. She put Diarmad to work shelling bright green peas while she made a rich leek soup and roasted spring lamb.

"You'd think it was Easter," Seán said as he breathed in the beautiful aromas.

"But it *is* Easter!" Brigid exclaimed with a laugh. "Today is Easter Sunday!"

Seán felt for the glove in his breast pocket and patted it tenderly. So much time had passed since he had left Thréig, he hadn't realized. He had come to love this little island family that had saved him—the little boy who had befriended him—but it was truly time to be on his way again to find his own boy.

That evening as they sat down to Brigid's sumptuous Easter feast, Diarmad picked at his food and barely spoke. He chased a lone pea around his plate with a butter knife and sighed deeply.

"He's sad that you're leaving," Brigid said, rubbing the boy's back.

"We all are," Angus said.

"It gets a wee bit lonely here sometimes on the island, except when the will of God and the Sea bring us friends," Brigid continued. "We'll always be glad that the storm left you here. Who knows but you'll find your way back to us again someday. You'll always be welcome."

*   *   *

Seán was ready to leave at dawn. Brigid could not watch him go, and Angus, having wished him a safe journey, stayed behind to comfort his wife. Only little Diarmad had come down to the shore with him to see him off. Seán strapped down his gear in the bow of the *Corncrake* and made ready to sail in the direction he felt certain he must go.

With all his preparations made, Seán looked back at the little boy sitting on a boulder, engulfed in the huge docile cat on his lap. Finn's yellow-green eyes were closed in ecstasy as the chubby little dimpled hands stroked him from head to tail in mournful farewell. What a calm, gentle child. Soft like Finn . . . like Callum . . . like he himself before life had hardened him. Seán had thought for a dreadful time that he'd lost everything he had ever loved—his wife, his son, his island, and nearly his boat. For a time, all he had left in the world was Finn, yet he knew then, in that moment, that Finn was no longer his to keep. Their friendship had been for a season only. They had helped each other, both in their own way, and their journey together was at an end.

"Finn's so soft," Diarmad cooed mournfully, pressing his round red cheek to the top of Finn's head.

"He is, isn't he? . . . would you like to keep him, Diarmad?"

The boy raised his head. His eyes grew wide with disbelief.

"It's just that he's so happy there in your arms, and I've never seen him so *un*happy as when we were at sea. That's where I must go again now, to go and find my Callum. Poor old Finn. Would you care for him for me, Diarmad? Would you make him your own friend and keep him safe from ever being so frightened again?"

"Yes," the boy said solemnly. "I will. I'll feed him little fishes and breadcrumbs and I'll make sure he purrs. I'll love him forever."

"And I can see he already loves you." Seán smiled and knelt down beside them. "Finn, my friend, you've been grand and brave. You've endured trials no cat should be expected to face, and you've been a good friend to me when I needed one most. I never knew how much I needed you. Let me

do this for you now." He scratched between Finn's large ears then rose to his feet. "Take care of each other," he said as he turned away from them, a slight ache rising in his throat.

It hurt. But it hurt far less to give away freely this last thing he loved— far less than having his loves taken from him by force. Seán reflected on that truth as he began to walk back toward the *Corncrake* and the next leg of his journey. Suddenly he felt Diarmad plucking at his sleeve. The boy, with great reverence and solemnity, unfolded Seán's rough old hand and placed a stone in its center. It was smooth, worn by countless tides, and nearly pure white. One of Diarmad's own well-loved treasures. Neither of them spoke a word but smiled knowingly as both understood the ritual, whose meaning bridged the chasm of age and culture: the mutual sacrifice of pure friendship.

7

T HE SEA WAS SO calm, like a slab of dark glass stretching into the blue distance. As if in one of his dreams, Seán pushed out from the quiet shore at Jura, waving to the little boy and the big gray cat who watched him leave. He rowed with long, steady pulls at the oars in the direction he knew he must go. Angus had given him detailed directions before he left, but Seán could have found his way to Iona with nothing but the tug he felt, as though he were a fish caught on a thin, invisible line being reeled inexorably toward his fate.

He made this journey alone—no angry cat to cling to him, or for him to talk to, as he made his way to Port na Curaich. That was the place Saint Columcille had first set foot on the Isle of Iona. The saint had climbed from that point up a high knoll and looked back toward his homeland. He knew he had journeyed far enough from Ireland when the land of his fathers was well and truly out of sight. Now Seán headed there with certainty that the place of Saint Columcille's exile was where he would find his boy at last. The certainty did not come from a place of reason or logic, but from a feeling in his bones so strong that it seemed irrefutable.

The unusually quiet waters whispered and lapped against the *Corncrake* as the oars reached—reached—reached—dragging at the water like a man swimming on his back. As Seán approached the rising dark grey headlands and gullies of Lewisian gneiss, the waters around the currach began to glow a luminous emerald green in the sunlit shallows. When he finally came upon Port na Curaich, he knew it, and it was right where it ought to be as if it had awaited his arrival for millennia, just as it had awaited the arrival of its own blessed saint centuries before. Seán pulled the currach to shore and drank in the silence, interrupted only by soft sea whispers, distant calls of seabirds, and the rising inner crescendo of utter certainty.

Seán propped up the currach as a lean-to shelter far enough up the shingle to be safe from the coming and going of the tide. That night was clear and shimmering with the ancient light of stars both familiar and strange. As he lay down to sleep, the drumming of the snipe filled the night, followed by the familiar rasp of the corncrake recently returned from its long winter sojourn. It gladdened his heart to hear them, and he smiled. He slept easily and deeply under the watchful luminaries and the shelter of his boat.

First light summoned the cuckoo's insistent call, joined eventually by the gentler tones of meadow pipit and skylark. Seán was surprised to find upon waking that he had no stiffness from sleeping on the ground. He rose feeling limber and young and ate with gratitude the tatty scones Brigid had sent with him for his journey. With those feelings of youth and strength came the remembrance of bare feet and of sand between the toes. Seán smiled at the memory, removed his boots, and rolled his trouser legs.

Walking along the shore in his bare feet in the early morning light, Seán noticed green pebbles of serpentine marble and cream-colored cowries scattered before his path where the tide had left them. He stooped to pick up one of the green pebbles, turning it over and over in his rough fisherman's fingers. Diarmad would have liked it—the shocking green. So would Callum. Seán felt the sudden urge to fill his trouser pockets with green stones and shiny pale shells, something he hadn't done since he was a boy, if he had ever done it at all. He walked slowly along, head down, scanning the shore for treasures, picking among the pebbles like the curlews and oystercatchers.

Green stones clopped and rattled in his pocket against the smooth white stone Diarmad had given him, and both pockets grew damp and heavy with bits of Ionian marble and shells. Seán sat himself down on an ice-age erratic of pink Ross of Mull granite, worn and weathered smooth. He reached into his pocket drawing forth a fistful of sandy beach treasures. He bent over them, sorting through them with his forefinger to choose the finest ones to keep. He took Muireann's Easter glove from his breast pocket and smiled as he put the prettiest rocks inside it as though placing the treasures in her hand. As he continued sorting through the heaps of pebbles and shells from his pockets, a stranger's deep voice met his ear from somewhere behind him.

"Collecting Saint Columcille's tears, Father?" Seán turned to see a face he didn't know, all covered in thick dark beard, brown and creased from the

sun. The stranger, a tough, rather dangerous-looking and weather-beaten man with fresh scars stood atop a low headland of gneiss looking down at him. *Father?* Seán thought. *The man thinks I'm a pilgrim priest.*

"So, these are they? I'm not a priest myself, sir, but I know one back in County Donegal who would be glad to have a Tear of Saint Columcille to call his own."

The man tilted his head to one side with an amused grin under his beard, crossing strong brown arms across his chest. He looked at Seán from one eye, then the other like a bird.

PART IV

The Father, the Son, and the Holy Island

1

"PEOPLE HAVE ALWAYS MADE pilgrimages to Iona, even while Saint Columcille was still living. He was known far and wide as a holy man, and people would travel great distances to see him. They would ask for his prayers or advice, and many men even wished to join his community. It got crowded, in fact, with all the visitors—the repentant and the curious—and the community on Iona was small. When they couldn't take on any more novices there, and their life of quiet isolation was becoming far too noisy, Saint Columcille had to travel out to other islands looking for places that were quiet enough to hear one's own prayers. He founded new monasteries since there were so many men in those days who had lived rough and violent lives and were looking for a bit of peace for their souls in the monastic vows.

"The curious, the penitent, and the pious still travel to Iona to see the place where our own great saint established his first monastic community in exile from his homeland. Maybe you'll see Iona someday. Would you like that? See the holy island where Saint Columcille set up his scriptorium, heard confessions, and visited with the angels? Wouldn't that be a blessing to see? Callum?"

The silence weighed massively on the room, a swelling, throbbing silence that badly wanted relief. A sound other than the relentless thud of blood in the ears. Callum sat on the floor cross-legged, his eyes fixed on a mottled brown feather that he twisted and twirled between his thumb and forefinger in front of his face. He looked at everything that way—long and careful and silent—until the thing itself would squirm if it could. Muireann squirmed on the feather's behalf, trying to shift that heavy, throbbing slab of silence herself.

"Do you think you might be drawn to the monastic life, Callum? Like your patron?"

Still the boy would not speak or lift his intense gaze from the feather, but twirled it more furiously between his fingers, making little breaths of wind come off it against his face.

"Or perhaps to the priesthood?" Muireann waited, her breathing shallow and expectant. The weight of his silence pressed on her own mind in the shape and substance of dread—the realization or admission of things half-known. Finally, Callum slowly shook his head.

Muireann searched her son's face. His brows were drawn together forming a serious little crease between them, just like his father's which was now a deep, permanent crag from years of habit and squinting against the sun. He kept his eyes still stubbornly fixed on the feather, turning it around and around, fluttering the soft downy barbs at the base of the rachis and catching air along the vane.

"You don't have to decide now," she said with a little wobble in her voice that she tucked behind a brave, but not altogether natural smile. "Sure, there's plenty of time."

"No," he said at last. "I've decided. I don't want to be exiled to a barren island far from home. I want *my* island. Where *my* people are. I want to be like Daddy. He prays just as good as any monk, but he loves his family. He works hard at the work he's chosen for himself, and at night he's not alone with a rock for a pillow. I want family and home and to choose my own work . . . work that's important. I want my island and my birds, my mother and my father. Someday I want my own family, and my own son or daughter will love me like I love Daddy. And when they spread their wings to leave me, I will cry like the seabirds, but I'll smile, too, because I'll remember when I left my parents, with gratitude . . . and with love. I won't be a monk or a priest. But I won't be a fisherman like Daddy, either. I'll do things in my own way, but even so, I'm my father's son, after all . . . why shouldn't I live a life just a little bit like his?" Callum paused and let the feather fall from his hand, watching it drift slowly down to the floor before finally meeting his mother's gaze. "Why are you crying? Mammy?"

"My boy . . . my darling wee bird . . ." Her voice wobbled and started to break as her eyes glistened with tears that soon spilled down her cheeks as she gazed at her miracle, sitting on the floor before her—growing so tall and so sure of his own mind. The child they had stopped looking for. Stopped hoping for. The child whose destiny she had seen with such clarity in her mind from the moment of his birth. "I had dreamed such things for

you," she said. "I had dreamed we'd *all* be so much more than we are . . . so much better."

"Am I bad, Mammy? To want these things? . . . Mammy?"

"There's plenty of time . . . you're still just a wee 'un. There's plenty of time. Best to wait on making big decisions until you've lived a little more." Muireann raised a rough red knuckle to her eye and swept away the rising, salty tide. "There's plenty of time."

* * *

"Callum?" Seán knew his son by that curious way he looked at him, tilting his head hawk-like to look at him first through one eye, then the other, taking him in from every possible perspective. The high-shouldered stoop which had always been the boy's shy habit, as though trying to make himself small and hard to see like a corncrake on its nest, had matured into the confident stance of a man more at home in his own skin. But those eyes! Those piercing falcon-eyes! He could never mistake them even under a bramble of unkempt hair!

The man on the rock unfolded his arms, strong and scarred from his own adventures and misadventures, and spread them out at his sides as though to catch an updraft.

"No, Callum! Don't fly away from your father! Not this time!"

Callum smiled and climbed down to Seán, wrapping strong featherless wings around the old man. They wept wordlessly on each other's shoulders. As Seán squeezed shut his eyes and held tight to his boy, he felt himself swept up on the breeze, swirled upon the salty air currents. He saw before his closed eyes the fierce yet kind eye of the bird that carried him in its gentle talons, floating and swooping over the sea with cries of bittersweet joy. Then he felt himself released, but he didn't fall. He opened his eyes to his Callum's smiling face.

Seán scraped and scoured the edges of his mind for those very important words he had wanted to say to his boy if ever he found him, but his mind felt as smooth and bleached as a whale's bone washed up onto the beach, and not a word would come to him. He cleared his throat with an unshaven growl as a sudden current of shame rushed over him, leaving a gray humming in his ears. He looked down at his sandy, bare feet.

"They're a wonder, aren't they? These green stones," Seán stammered at last, holding out his fistful of smooth Ionian marble.

"Indeed, they are. Though I can't say I've ever known my father to be a great collector of stones and beach treasures."

"Men can change when they learn to own their faults. And I've been learning a great many of my own these past years. A great many, to my everlasting shame. I've also promised to take one of these home to the priest who blessed my journey here, and my boat. That's her down the beach." Seán gestured toward the *Corncrake*, still upturned and resting on the shingle. A few curious curlews poked around in the shadows underneath it. "I built it for us."

"Us? You and me?"

"It was a foolish thought, I know. Treacly and sentimental, but I had it in my head to take you to Toraigh Island and see all the wee pufflings in their burrows, and that bunch of corncrakes that you used to talk about. I thought we could travel all around the little islands together seeing new birds and new shores, just the two of us. To explore and to know this world and each other better."

"So . . . she *has* died, then," Callum said, his eyes still resting on the sleek black form of the boat basking on the sunny shore like a wet harbor seal.

"Yes . . . yes, so she has."

"When?"

"September last."

Callum's face seemed more confused than aggrieved, and he appeared to have trouble controlling its waves of expression.

"September! That long?"

"I tried to reach you."

"I was in Africa in September."

"I know."

"I thought . . . there was a moment, you see, just a few weeks or so ago. I felt death, or at least I thought I did. I truly thought it was her leaving. The anguish of it! I was so certain. But she was already gone?"

"Yes, and peaceful was her passing. No anguish. Death rolled in on the tide, and carried her away with it, gentle-like. A perfect death, if such a thing isn't blasphemous to say. It hurt me far more than it hurt her, I think. A Christian ending: 'painless, blameless, and peaceful; and with a good defense before the dread judgment seat of Christ.'"

"Dread judgment . . . some face it before their end. Well, I don't know what I felt then, that night. It was as though a great gaping hole had been

punched through my heart with the haft of an oar. Ripping and rending its way through my center. I felt that way only once in my life before. . . I thought it was her. I would have sworn to it. Surely, I've disappointed no one in this world more than her."

"It was me. I did it. It was I who drove an oar through the very heart of my boat when I had the letter last month that told me you'd died. Punched a hole clean through her . . . for that was how I felt. Broken and empty of all regret. I thought I'd lost everything."

"They told you I died? I'm sorry . . . administrative incompetence is nearly as predictable as the corncrake's migration. I'm so sorry for the pain that must have caused you."

"I nearly gave up with that letter. I came so close! But I decided to come anyway to see if you might still be alive somewhere undiscovered. And I had things to say to you. Things I should've told you long ago. Only now I can't think of a single one of them except that I'm sorry . . . I'm *sorry* . . . " Seán searched his son's face, wishing, willing to find relief and forgiveness there, but all he saw was confusion and pain.

"My mother has been dead these eight months . . . and you were told I was dead as well? But you built a sailing currach, left everything you knew behind, and came looking for me yourself?"

"Your mother . . . she's at peace now. I needed to find some peace myself."

"At peace—I hope that's true, at least for one of us."

"Oh Callum! I'll spend the rest of my days making up for the ways I've failed you, son! I will! I know I don't deserve forgiveness, but in the name of Saint Columcille and all the blessed saints—"

"But that's it exactly! Don't you see? The *name* of Saint Columcille! The blessed *name*." Callum's eyes bored into Seán like flaming embers.

"The name?" Seán asked.

"I *know* Saint Columcille's name is important. I *feel* it's important. My mother made sure I knew it was important. And knowing it, bearing that parentage has been the heaviest of burdens."

"Your name a burden? But why? It's just a name."

"No, it's not just a name. Our names show the world the truth about us. The name that parents give a child may not be the one he would have chosen for himself, but it sets him upon a current. Whether he wants to go that way or not, the current bears him eventually to the *reason* for his name."

"I don't understand." Seán searched his son's grave, weathered face. It was deeply carved with the cares and worries of years that Seán hadn't seen. Troubles Seán hadn't been there to share. How many of those worries had he himself caused his son to carry with him through these past years? "The *reason* for your name? Is that what's troubling you?"

"The *Dove*, father—the Dove of the *Church*. I know the stories so well I feel I've lived them because that was *her* gift. Making story into something that feels like preconscious memory. Her own peculiar magic was with words, and her stories all became personal truths in their own way. Didn't she see herself as Eithne, who was given the vision of her child's spiritual greatness? Who raised him to become the saint who was foretold? Was she not the mermaid who rescued the fisherman from the sea serpent? The mermaid who married the fisherman and became a saint?

"She wove me into the tale as Saint Columcille, who had to migrate far from his ancestral land to make his peace with God. She made me the Dove's far-distant Godchild, bearing his name and his love for his own homeland. Only the true exile of the story was the corncrake. And I followed it. Went chasing after it from our land to this one. Do you not see? I've always been chasing after my name, living this life like an echo. No matter how I live, I look back behind me and the story is following me. I follow my name and it follows me.

"The chase led me nearly to my death before it led me here, to his island and my name." Callum smiled at his father, tenderly now. "You know, it wasn't really 'Jonah' I'd have called myself if I'd had the chance to choose. Jonah was just the same, you know, and Columcille was *his* godchild. No, if I could have chosen my own name, I'd have taken yours."

"Mine?" Seán said incredulously.

"Yes."

"But why?"

"Why? Because I only ever wanted to be like my father. A man, not a myth."

Seán's eyes began threatening to leak tears again and he reached. He reached back far into the murk of his own memories. Why hadn't he named his son after himself? He knew very well, though the words were difficult to assemble. He held them carefully in his mind, shaping them like wood into their truest form before he dared to speak them.

"Seán was *my* father's name. Maybe it would have been proper and natural to give it to you, as he gave it to me. I can see now how that might

have made things easier for you, especially with all the expectations that come with more storied names, though there's been many a fisherman named John, and not all of them fished for fish. I could have given you my name, I suppose . . . "

"Why didn't you? Was I not deserving of my father's name?"

"No, lad. It wasn't for lack of deserving, or for lack of love that I didn't give you my name, and my father's before me. You're right . . . you're right that a man's name is a burden to him no matter who the man was who had it first. I wanted to set you free from mine."

"Free?"

"You know, when you left, it surprised me how much it hurt to let you go. I regret not sending you off with my blessing. I regret the harsh words I did say to you. But your *name!* Your name itself was always meant to be just that: your blessing to leave me. The blessing I never had, nor ever dared to seek." Seán heard his own words and knew they were true because they smote him with regret.

"You see, even with my father's name, it is only *now*—now that I'm old—that I can finally say I've entered into the brotherhood of my fathers. I've only just realized that my life was always mine for the making. But you, Callum—you took your life and claimed your place in the brotherhood of your fathers while your *own* father was still just a son toiling in his dead father's field. I may regret many things, but I regret most that I didn't send you with my wordiest and proudest blessing when I had the chance. But to be sure, it was a blessing you never really needed . . . *because* of your name."

2

T HE LATE SPRING SUN rose high in the sky and beat overhead, a clear
and unseasonably warm noonday blaze, as the two men sat on Iona's
green-speckled shore staring at one another. The younger pulled a small
loaf of bread, some slightly sweaty cheese, and a flask of tea from his satchel
and the two shared it between them.

"Why Callum, though? Why tie me to Saint Columcille at all? Was that
all my mother?" the young man asked, brushing crumbs from his beard.

"No, we chose it together, your mother and me. She loved the stories, it's true, and knew them better than I did. But son, you're not named
Columcille. You're named *Callum*. You aren't the Dove of the Church,
you're simply the *Dove*. Surely that makes all the difference, doesn't it? It's
the dove that brings peace and truth on its wings. The more I think of it,
the name in itself *was* a prophecy, as you say. But a prophecy your mother
didn't recognize for what it was, so taken was she with the old story that
she didn't see the new one unfolding. What better name for a man who
loves the birds as you do? You lived up to your name from the day I saw
you perched up on the cliff loving every bird you saw. You're deserving of
the name. Yes, maybe your mother placed a bit more hope and expectation
in its reference to the saint she loved, but for *my* part, your name was only
ever meant to make you free of *me*, and it's a name that suits you better than
mine ever could have."

Callum stared out at the waves as they lapped at the shingle, tossing
and tumbling green stones in the foam. The air was heavy with the sea's
whispers.

"Freedom is a fearful thing," he said at last. "I wanted it—God knows,
I longed for it. But it's like being on the open sea in a very small boat. And
I, without my strong fisherman father who knew the sea better than I. I've
wanted you a thousand times. . .one time most desperately."

"You've wanted *me*? Surely it was your mother who was always the guiding star for you. How you clung to her and her stories . . . her magic and her warmth. What help have I ever been to you? I never wanted to hold you back, but I have anyway. I know I have, and I'm sorry for it. At least your mother was always a safe harbor to you."

"Yes . . . " Callum stared at the horizon, his brow knit and his jaw muscles working themselves aimlessly.

"Why didn't you come, Callum? Why didn't you come straight home from Jura?"

"How did you know I was there?" Callum asked, turning to Seán, wonderment in his falcon-eyes.

"I washed up there, too. I met that wee family. The goddess Brigid worked her healing magic one me as she did on you, and her man Angus helped me repair my currach. This stone here in my pocket is from our young Master Diarmad." Seán handed the smooth white stone to Callum, who smiled and turned the stone over in his hand. "Why didn't you come straight home from there?"

Callum's smile faded, his face contorting into an expression of pure torment.

"I don't know how to say it. It's a feeling. A terrible, terrible feeling of disapproval and disappointment. She wanted to raise a saint—a monk, a priest, a holy martyr even. Maybe you meant for my name to be freedom, but she meant it as a holy calling and a duty. Yes, my mother was a safe harbor and a guiding star. I loved her just as you say. I felt . . . I still feel there was something extraordinary about her, even approaching genius. But Da . . . it's not *your* blessing I've been wanting all these years. It's *hers*."

Seán's heart fluttered against his rib cage like something trying to break free. He sucked a great gusting gasp into his lungs that went straight to his head as his mind seemed to tilt and seize as though filling with cold seawater. He grasped at his son's arm.

"Da! Are you all right?" Callum grasped his father's shoulder and held two fingers to the pulsing artery under the old man's jaw.

"Son . . . you don't know. You can't know how many years . . ." He slowed his breathing, resting his forehead on Callum's shoulder until the world came right again. "I've thought a great many things, Callum. But I never thought . . ."

"No. You wouldn't think it. You weren't there," there was a reluctance in his voice as he observed his father's face, pinched and withered with

weather and grieving. "You told her, 'Callum is leaving. Make sure he has what he needs.' Do you remember? That was enough for me. You didn't argue. You didn't try and stop me. You told me I was a damned fool for leaving, but you never tried to stop me. Then you left with your pipe. You left me alone with my mother."

"What happened when I left? What did she say to you?"

Callum examined his father's face, concern creasing his brow.

"Come up to my tent. We need to get you out of the sun and get some water in you."

"But I need to know . . ."

"I know. You will. But you're wilting and need reviving."

Climbing up the rocky slope from the shore, the two men slowly crested the mounds, pausing to look out in the direction of Ireland, invisible, yet palpably present like the memory of something loved. They hiked slowly the monotonous grandeur of weather-beaten grass and granite and old stone walls to a more or less sheltered natural swale where a canvas tent stood next to a ring of stones that held the ashes of recent fires. Callum made his father lie down on his sleeping bag and brought him a cup of water from a large jug. Seán sipped the water and started to smile. The smile erupted into a chuckle, the like of which he hadn't experienced in years.

"What is it?" Callum asked.

"Is this how you've been living? Is this normal accommodation for a bird scientist?"

"Well, it's pretty typical for when I'm in the field. I've sat for hours in makeshift blinds perched on the sides of cliffs or out in the middle of boggy fields in the rain, wrapped in that sleeping bag and every piece of clothing I had just for warmth. But it's all worth it for the data I've been able to collect."

Seán's chuckle expanded into a deep, honest laugh as he sloshed water from his cup down his shirtfront.

"I'm sorry son, I was just thinking about how saintly and ascetical your life is. Exposed to the elements, sleeping on bare lonely islands without a proper roof over you, shivering on a rock just to count and study the birds. Like Adam the first man given the job of naming the beasts and caring for them."

"Saint Bird-Shite, indeed," Callum said with an ironic grin that smote Seán clean through the heart and banished the smile from his face.

"I hate my words to you that day. I cursed you to this discomfort and unhappiness. My words are powerful poison. I know that now."

"No, no. No, I love my work. I love it. I wouldn't want it any other way. And you're right. There's something of the ascetic life in it. A man has time enough on his hands to think a great many thoughts, to pray a great many prayers in a rain blasted bird blind. Your words aren't as powerful as all that. That is to say, I don't feel like it was you who poisoned me that day."

"But what did she *say* to you, son?"

Callum sighed as he sat cross-legged on the ground by his father.

"Well . . . she cried initially. Said it wasn't what she wanted for me at all. She talked of Saint Columcille and of lives devoted to prayer and the way of pilgrims, heroes, and saints. Said I was selling myself short and refusing my God-given destiny. She talked of my purpose and my vocation. She told me I'd broken her heart, that she'd only got the one child, and that she wished now she'd had none at all, if I was to squander my calling in such a thankless manner."

"I didn't know."

"She never talked of it?"

"No. All she ever said was that she guessed you'd be back eventually."

"Back eventually? She told me she didn't care to see me again."

"She . . . but the clothes! When you left you had new clothes and looked for all the world as though she'd dressed you for your future!"

"That was Miss Alexander again. My mother sent me with nothing but the assurance that I'd disappointed her. I'd have been home with you every holiday if I'd thought I was wanted."

"But you were! You were wanted! Needed! I never meant what I said, and I know she didn't either. You know why she went on about Saint Columcille's temper the way she did? It was because she knew what it was to have one herself! She was waiting for you. She said you'd be back, and that there was plenty of time."

"That's what she always said, though. *Sure, there's plenty of time.* That I was still just a wee'un, with *plenty of time.* I'd told her long before then that I wanted something else for my life. I *had* decided. A long time ago I'd decided, but she could never see it. She always expected one day I'd be having a vision or a dream that called me to the priesthood—to a monastery. What she didn't know was that I *did* have a vision. But it wasn't a vision she would've understood."

"You had a vision? . . . did you see the angels?"

"No. No angels. I saw the future, and it frightened me. I saw a dead land full of bones. I saw forests with no trees, skies with no birds, seas with

no fish, and families with no food. I saw roads leading nowhere, and nowhere to go even if the roads would take you there. I saw death, and it frightened me."

"Oh . . . that one. I've seen it," Seán said gravely.

"I know you have. You know the sea. You know what it is, and what it used to be even in your own lifetime. You taught me. Maybe you didn't mean to, but you taught me nonetheless. I don't believe my mother ever saw what was coming. Sometimes I wonder if she saw this world at all."

"No, not much of it. I'll own I protected her from it. I didn't want her worrying about things that wouldn't come to pass in her lifetime. She'd suffered enough. I didn't want to tarnish her magic with too much reality," Seán said.

"Yes . . . magic. You may not feel like you gave me your blessing, but I somehow felt I had it nonetheless, because we are the same. We are men of earth, and sea, and sky. My mother was something else entirely. She was magic, spirit, and holiness . . . the *other*world. You might have thought my plans were impractical, but I knew in the end you would understand them. I'm not sure she could have. And I could never bear her disapproval."

"I think she did understand in the end. At least a little. I think she began to see those worlds merging even as she left this one. I wish you could have come and seen her before . . ." "I know. I wish the same. I wish I'd had your letters, and I'm sorry you've had to bear it all alone. But you asked me why I didn't come straight home from Jura. That's why. The feeling that I was unworthy to come home to my mother's grave. So I came here instead—the Holy Island—to try at least to ease the sense of disappointment I *still* felt from her, even from beyond the grave. I could justify being here because of the birds, and because of my name. I couldn't justify going home."

Seán's tears now flowed unchecked and unheeded with an unexpected mixture of sorrow and relief.

"But what is it you've been doing here all this time?"

Callum looked at his father's face, strained, gray, and weary from too many tears, too little water, and long hours of exposure.

"I'll show you soon, but rest for now."

3

SEÁN WASN'T AWARE OF closing his eyes. Sleep took him, without his having to strive for it, and kept him through the rest of that day and the night that followed. His thoughts contorted and shifted in shape and substance, but never fully faded away. His mind was full of words and images. He paced the restless shores of his dreams, that corridor he'd often visited in search of comforting memories in the past months of his grief. This time he searched for something he knew wasn't there. It couldn't be because it wasn't a memory at all. It was something he knew had never been, could never be, but he must try to find it nonetheless and this was the only place he knew to look.

He felt along the invisible web that formed the boundary between this place and all the others. He felt for an opening that might lead into the one place he needed to be. All he needed was to find a thin spot that he might stretch and tear and press himself through. He floated soundless and soft through the thick warmth of that other place until he met a resistance that felt different from the others, more firm, yet this one didn't wish to be noticed. He could only sense its presence when he wasn't looking at it directly. He fixed his focus on the silent sea that flanked the shore of dreams and pushed his hand against that secret barrier that warped and shimmered in the corner of his vision like heat rising.

It was diaphanous but durable and repelled him when he pressed it. He pushed against it harder, running his hands along the surface, searching for some gap that he could widen and push his way through. He searched for what felt like ages, but he knew that he couldn't stop. He dug his fingers into the web-like barrier that kept him on that side of consciousness until his fingers were stiff and cramped. He looked before him through the thing that did not wish to be seen, rested his head against it, this resistance without substance, and waited.

"You can't come in this way," her voice said from the other side, distant and echoing. "It's not a proper entrance."

"I don't know of any other."

"Yes you do. But that one isn't open to you yet."

"I'm glad you came. This will do just as well," he said.

"You look tired."

"I am. I've been exploring, just as you told me."

"What have you discovered?"

"I've discovered wonders."

"Tell me about them."

"I found another man's son who'd been cursed and cut down, but who still found it in his heart to forgive. He taught me to hope that I might be forgiven, too. I found a lonely barren island where a father is learning to heal ground spoilt by those who came before, where a mother heals lost broken men, and where a child runs and plays with a cat who repays its debts. I found friends. I found tears that heal, and I found green stones. I found a strong, brave man who used to be my child, but now he's my brother."

"What did he tell you when you finally found him?"

"He told me everything, Muireann." Seán heard a sound like a sigh without breath, without wind. An airless, voiceless keening that wound its way through his mind cold and dry before fading into peace and release.

"Tell him that he was—is—and ever shall be loved by his mother."

"I'll tell him."

"Pride is a fearful thing . . . but love will always be stronger." Her voice was long and stretched thin like the receding tones of far distant angelus bells. It stretched and faded into the dark. Sean's mind grew heavier until, ever so gently, it closed.

* * *

Seán opened his eyes to the first rays of late-spring sunshine glimmering through the weave of Callum's tent. He raised his head to see that he was alone inside, but close by he heard the soft crackle of a fire, and the clink of a metal pot. He peaked his head out of the flap to see Callum boiling water for tea, and toasting buns over a small fire. He turned to smile at his father, the pure, sweet smile he'd carried on his face as a boy wandering the fields

after secretive birds, finding their feathers, nests, and fragments of speckled shell.

"You look better. You must be half-perished with hunger, though." He handed Seán one of the hot buns that had been caught least by the flames and poured tea into two tin cups sighing steam into the cool morning air.

"Is this a typical bird-scientist's breakfast?"

Callum laughed.

"This is quite grand, actually. I normally just have the tea and get down to work, but you need a bite of something in you. Have you not been eating at all?"

"I have so! More than usual as I can never remember to make just the one bowl of porridge!" Seán found he could laugh about that now. What a difference a few months and near-death at sea could make!

"Well, you eat up your nice breakfast and we'll see if you feel up to some field work."

"Field work, is it? What can need harvesting at this time of year?"

"Data of course!"

"Are we counting birds?"

"Counting nests and eggs per nest for now. Did you know that Iona has one of the largest corncrake breeding colonies in the UK? They arrived last month, come up from wintering in Mozambique. I spent the greater part of the winter watching them there."

"That's quite a distance to travel for a little brown bird."

"Yes. Much farther than Saint Columcille journeyed to get here. But exiles both in their way. He was banished from his homeland—they were banished from the mainland."

"But what good am *I* to you? If it was swinging a scythe or hauling up lobster creels I might be of use, but . . ."

"All you need is a light, careful step, and a keen eye. I'll show you what to look for and what to do once you've found it. Now get that tea into you and mind you eat your whole bun. We've an awful lot of walking ahead of us this morning."

They sipped their tea too quickly, scalding their tongues, and wrapped the remaining buns in a sack for later. Callum outfitted his father with binoculars and a flask of water, and they set off. Callum held a detailed map of the island, much weather-worn and scribbled with notes and strange markings. He showed Seán the areas where he had already recorded breeding pairs, and how many eggs were in each clutch.

"They're a secretive bird and they live a mostly hidden life skulking about in the tall grass, reedbeds, and irises. We'll try and cover this area today," Callum said, tracing his forefinger over a small portion of the map. "They keep grassy little ground nests that you might not see until you're right on top of them, so you must move slowly and cautiously. The mother will be loath to abandon her eggs even as you approach her. They've been known to stay protecting their clutches even as big tractors and harvesters roll right over them, crushing them and their eggs with them."

"They're stubborn and stick to their land. I like that about them."

"Yes. We might need to gently convince the mother to leave her eggs for just long enough so that we can make an accurate count. It might be easier at night when she's gotten up to find herself some beetles or snails, but I haven't got the funding for night vision, and it's too bulky to be practical anyway."

"Night vision?"

"Like soldiers use, to find the enemy in the dark, only I can think of a hundred better uses for it in my line of work. Can you imagine if we could use it to find nocturnal creatures and observe them without disturbing them? Everything in nature behaves differently when it knows it's being watched. We can only determine the adaptive significance of behavior when we can be sure that the behavior itself is natural and not influenced by the very instruments we use to collect our data. We've got a long way to go, but things are changing."

Seán listened silently. What did it all mean? And here he'd been thinking that the boy watched birds because they were pretty and could fly. Here he'd been picturing his son blithely collecting feathers and drawing pictures and probably earning his bread giving museum tours to school children.

"So," he said carefully, "you don't watch the birds just to admire them, like? There are things you want to know and reasons why you would need to know them?"

"Of course I admire them. Admiration is the beginning for most people. What child hasn't dreamed of flying? What mind doesn't marvel to watch the fulmar coasting and swooping over the white caps on a rough wind, or a guillemot diving six hundred feet into the ocean for its food? Life on the wing is majestic and mysterious. Of course I admire them, but admiration can only go so far. Admiration has led to a lot of sentimental thinking about birds, which hasn't been all bad, but sentiment alone is a dangerous basis for conservation."

"Sparing a bird because there's a good song about it, you mean?"

"Yes, exactly. When you sing of blackbirds in the nursery, they become important. When a poem extols the beauty of the nightingale's song, one doesn't think of eating her. Imagine if we only cared for the most beautiful animals and plants? The ones we understand best and which, through our own imagination, have come to represent human traits that we admire. What if we protected only the birds of our favorite color, or the mammals without sharp teeth and claws? The ones that don't get in our way, that don't smell bad or steal from us—don't lie to chickens or swallow our grannies whole? What if we bring in new species that we like to hunt or to eat, and eradicate the ones that ought to be here to keep the land healthy and balanced? Imagine a forest with no fox, lynx, or wild cat. An ocean with no sharks. No, but you needn't imagine, because that's the growing reality. We can't pick and choose what creatures deserve to stay. We need them all in right proportion."

"But *you've* picked the corncrake. Is it not your favorite?"

"It is," Callum smiled. "I watch a lot of birds, depending on the season and the funding. I watch mostly seabirds, following their migrations and recording their numbers, for we can judge the health of the sea partly by the health of those creatures who live off its produce. So I count them. Band them. Watch them. I watch them descend in great shrieking shoals on the same reeking breeding cliffs every year to raise their young. And every year I watch the numbers fall a little more. Not for all of them, but for most. I watch fulmars, shearwaters, kittiwakes, puffins . . . but you're right that I care for corncrakes most of all. I care for them because they're homely, brown, speckled, and secretive. Birds of pasture and meadow. They live their lives in hiding, not asking to be looked at and admired. They might not be noticed at all, unless you know to look for them. I care for them most because they remind me of my father."

"Of me?"

"I've watched my father cling to his native soil and way of living even as his species dies out around him or is displaced and forced to adapt to a changing environment. He sits stubbornly on his nest even as modern life rolls over him and threatens to destroy everything he's built. Everything he's loved. Even as the big industrial fishing operations strip the oceans of his food and his livelihood. And as time and illness steals away his mate. My father is a stubborn, secretive brown bird."

"Maybe. But everything and everyone has their time. Maybe mine and the corncrake's is ending. You can't stop the tide once it's turned."

"Maybe not. Then again, only a century ago kittiwakes were still being shot in the thousands every year for sport and for decorating ladies' hats. Scores of millions of birds were killed for their feathers before the plumage trade was finally stopped through the tireless efforts of people both in my profession and out of it making a ruckus. But it is still far easier to make people *feel* something for the big beautiful noticeable birds. To make them want to *do* something. If the mute swan was in danger, whole communities would rise up to save it because it makes them think of starlit romantic evenings and stolen kisses. But what about the little brown birds that nobody sees? It is easy to live one's life blind to the importance of creatures with such separate destinies, such self-contained existences. They are the island folk and small boat fishermen and otherworldly storytellers. They will continue to disappear quietly, and their absence will only be felt on summer nights when their ratcheting calls no longer fill our dreams. We will only know the extent of their value to the land and our own lives once they're gone, and then it will be too late."

4

THE EARLY MORNING SUN shone fair on the two men as they slowly stalked the reedy hummocks and pastures of Iona in search of secret nests. Callum found the first and showed his father what to look for. Perhaps his eyes were simply not as keen as they used to be, but Callum kept finding nests Seán never saw until he was right next to them. He watched as his son made careful note of their position on the map and recorded the number of eggs in swift, efficient marks. Callum worked with seriousness and urgency, but also with a contagious sense of joy. Every nest was gold, and every egg was a gem. Seán learned to see them that way as well. An unexpected feeling of pride and pleasure welled up in him upon finding his first nest. The mother's shiny black eyes stared at him suspiciously through the tall reeds.

He saw her, still as a stone, huddled on her grassy nest with her head nestled down between her shoulders. Her dappled brown feathers would have easily hidden her from an eye not looking for her. He crept slowly toward her, trying to see how many eggs she hid under her breast. He saw at least three, cream colored with dark brown speckles. One of them looked damaged with long spidery cracks along its thin wall. Seán waved, motioning to Callum, who picked his way over though the rushes and reeds.

"She has at least three," Seán whispered, "but there's something wrong with one of them. Do you count them still if they're broken?"

Callum looked long at the damaged egg through the magnification of his binoculars. A smile slowly crept though the bearded thicket on his face and he motioned for Seán to kneel next to him. Callum placed a hand on his father's shoulder and whispered into his ear.

"It's hatching. Watch."

As they sat there barely breathing, the thin, spidering cracks continued to spread and grow until a nubby little black beak tip peaked from the

epicenter. How long it seemed to take. How long they sat there on the damp ground watching this tiny, monumental event. And how shocking it must be, Seán thought, when the creature was finally free. All the chick had ever known, the boundaries of its existence were that shell and the warmth of its mother's breast radiating through it. What a terrible shock the world must be to that poor wet weeping babe. What a terrible shock when you find that everything you've ever known is thin and shattering about you. How unsafe it must feel, but oh, the wideness and the wonder of everything beyond that fragile shell that was safety only for a season!

"It's black! Like a little ball of soot!" Seán whispered, as the dark downy feathers began to dry and fluff. "I never knew they looked like that."

"Not many people do. It's a rare sight, even when you're looking for it. It won't look that way for long, though. Corncrake chicks are precocious. It will be flying before you know it."

By the time the sun was directly overhead, Callum folded up the map and led Seán to a shady spot to eat their buns. Beads of perspiration stood out on their foreheads and bits of grass and seed clung to the weave of their clothing. They rested in silence, listening only to the music of wind through waving reeds and birds. Callum would interject occasionally to tell Seán which bird's voice he was hearing, differentiating between calls for a mate, calls of alarm, and calls of simple avian pleasure. Callum spoke of the language of birds like a skilled interpreter, and Seán marveled not only at the depth of his son's knowledge, but that his own life had been filled with songs and language that held actual meaning. That a complex world and society had existed in parallel to his own without his ever taking much notice of it.

"*Umwelt*," Callum explained, in a wistful way. "The sensory universe of each unique species, known only to it. We live out our subjective experience in our own little worlds of meaning, barely realizing the depth and profundity of the lives and societies of those around us. It seems like we will always be at least partially blind to the significance of their world. It's hard enough to understand others of our own kind. To understand the experience of a man on a different continent, a different island, a different patch of earth just across from our own. How can we fathom the struggles and triumphs of our neighbor, even our own kin? Our own minds are all we can be really sure of, and even they can be overcast and hard to read. But we try. We must . . . we must try, nonetheless."

Callum stared into the blue distance as though his own mind had slipped into another creature's meaning-world and was trying to put what he saw there into his own language—or perhaps to create the language he was lacking. Words for all the meanings. He inhaled sharply and shook himself back into the present with the unfulfilled look of a guillemot whose deep dive proved fishless.

"Well, I'd like to show you something this afternoon, if you feel up to it," Callum said, finally dusting crumbs from his beard and taking a drink from his flask. "It's a different kind of creature entirely from the ones we've been stalking this morning. But this one's not so hard to find."

After a short rest, they rose and hiked inland through a scattering of blooming celandines, primroses, and wild hyacinths, harbingers at the margin of winter and spring. They trekked along old stone walls, across patches of moorland with creeping willow and juniper, and past gullies thick with stunted oak, hazel, and alder. As they crested a rise in the land, Seán saw the walls of a grand old edifice rise up before him—all pitched rooftops and pointed arches, the purple flowers of ivy leaved toadflax winking out of cracks between the stones.

"What is this?" Seán asked.

"It's Iona Abbey. It was built on the site of Saint Columcille's monastery." Callum led the way to the northwest side of the Abbey buildings. "Look. This earthen bank just here was part of the original site. Some say it was here even before Saint Columcille arrived with his companions. His buildings would have been mere wattle and timber, so they've disappeared with time and weather, but remnants have been found here and there. Remains of the place where he worked and wrote and lived out his exile."

"This is grand," Seán said staring down at the bank and imagining the saint writing by candlelight with a quill and embellishing the margins with bright mineral swirls, twisting knots, and fearsome creatures of the imagination. "She would have liked to see this. She would like that we came here together, you and me. Thank you. Thank you for showing me."

"It's why I came, really. Instead of going home. Well, this and the corncrakes. I wanted to see the place where he lived and did his work. Wanted to visit this site not just for me, but for her, supposing the departed can look in on us from time to time. I wanted to somehow show her that I did hear her stories and do carry them with me, in my way. I think it would ease her mind to know I've not forgotten it all . . . or her. I thought we could leave a wee cairn in her memory. Just a few stones here. Would you help me?"

Seán nodded and stooped to pick up a flat stone.

"Three," Seán said. "Three stones for the three of us." He placed the first stone, Callum the second, and together they placed the third, for Muireann. Seán rested his hand, lingering on the third stone. "Your mother loved you more than anything else in this world, Callum. She always did. She always will. She would be proud of you, just as I am. Proud of what you've done with your life and your name. What better mission could a man set for himself than to give his own life and comfort in sacrifice for what he knows is right, whether his own people understand it or not?"

5

THE SPRING PASSED BEFORE their eyes, even as the successful eggs hatched—the healthy corncrake chicks grew and fledged and flew. June 9th brought Saint Columcille's feast day, and they lent their hands along with many other pilgrims, to the ongoing restorations at the Abbey. The structure looked just a bit more whole than when they had arrived, but it would be many seasons toil until it looked as it had when it was new. But Seán and Callum had set stones there in Muireann's memory, and felt their own hearts restored a little as well in the process.

Then one gentle late-summer morning, dawn saw the *Corncrake* pulling out from Port na Curraich and tacking south, even as the corncrakes themselves and their precocious children were beginning to feel that inward tug toward Mozambique. A soul looking out from the Mounds would have seen an old-fashioned sailing currach on the horizon, its square sail billowing out before it, the dark silhouette of a hale old fisherman at the stern. In the bow they would have seen the outline of a younger man scanning with a pair of binoculars that misty line where white dawn skies meet the sea, watching the lift and dip of a few shearwaters in their low flight over the swelling waves, his hand outstretched and pointing. Two brothers on a voyage.

They sailed through fair weather and calm seas past the Fanad Head Lighthouse, past Lough Swilly and Sheep Haven. They sailed by Horn Head and Callum agreed—it did look like a monster from one of Muireann's stories. Finally, the two pulled ashore at Toraigh in time to see to see the August pufflings fledge. They watched the youngsters march from the safety of their underground burrows, hurling themselves from the cliffsides, never doubting the loving embrace of the sea that would catch them and care for them, each one solitary in its own winter pilgrimage.

"They certainly seem to know where they're off to," Seán observed.

"They're extraordinary creatures . . . what I wouldn't give for such instinct. Such intelligence. Each goes its own way in winter, not in a flock as some birds do. Each follows its own path, yet it goes the same way every time."

A heavy question had been looming unasked since spring, always set aside for later, until *later* became the unavoidable present. For now they had watched the majority of Toraigh's migrants leave in flocks for warmer climates—others for the winter seas and its riches. And yet the two of them lingered there in the growing quiet of the cliffside, and September had caught them up.

"Will you come back to Dublin with me?" Callum asked at last one evening. "I've got a position there waiting for me, now they know I'm not dead. I'd like to have you with me if you'll come."

Seán had known the day was coming when both Callum and his birds would fly away south, but he hadn't let himself plan beyond that one summer and never pictured himself making that journey with his son. He stared at their campfire, its feathers of golden light ruffling in the breeze that carried hints of chill autumn on its wings.

"I can't," he said at last.

"Can't . . . or won't?"

"I don't belong in the city, Callum."

"Nor do I, but it's not all bad. There are some lovely parks where you can feel more alone—less hemmed in by the bustle and the buildings. I'm bound to travel a lot for projects anyway. Out to remote areas—islands. You could come with me, and we could travel back to Thréig on my holidays. We'd barely be in the city at all."

"Callum, you are the best and kindest son a man could have. Let me do for you what I always should have and send you into your future with my blessing." He laid his brown, weather-hardened hand on Callum's head. "May God grant you joy in your work, and may you live to see the fruit of your labors. May you carry His truth and His presence into the busy world that rushes like waves to shore. And at the turning of the tide, may He always bring you back to your old father, and to the Holy Island. Let that be our meeting place."

"From the landing of the corncrakes to their leaving?"

"I'll be there."

"And where will you winter? On your island all alone?"

"Well, son, there's lots of islands out there, one with a cat and a little boy I'll need to check up on from time to time . . . and my *Corncrake* was built for exploring. I really think the man who built her may be more of a puffin at heart. A traveler on his own journey through winter, making his way toward the assurance of a warm reunion at the season's turning."

Callum smiled and reached his arm over his father's shoulder as they watched the fire burn down to embers.

"Then go with my blessing, too, into your own adventures and explorations. My father—my brother—my friend."

The next morning, the two of them packed up their camp and let the tide bring them home together that short remaining distance to the rosebush on the lonely western cliff of Thréig.

6

WHEN THE LAST OF the Thréig fishermen had sailed in the direction of his destiny that one early spring dawn, only one man knew the truth of his quest and the extent of its danger. Father Martin knew in his heart of hearts that he would never see Seán again, and that knowledge wounded the young priest with a profound sense of grief. When he came back to the mainland from his last day on the island, back to all his usual duties and nice habits, Father Martin was different. His eyes and his manner betrayed a softness that seemed less feigned—a sweetness more real as it had at its heart the slight bitter note that comes from loss—and an aloofness that, naturally, made all the twilight folk of the village seek him out.

Whatever the change or its cause, the whole parish noticed and felt suddenly moved by their young priest's seeming melancholia. They began showing up to Mass more or less on time—coming to vespers—to confession. Some even came by the priory that spring just to pay their respects and spend a half hour pulling weeds in the recently neglected vegetable patch. Mrs. Kelly was moved to baking cream cakes and biscuits, and hardly a Friday went by when someone did not bring Father Martin some plump, choice fish for his supper. Still, Father Martin gazed out at the western horizon most evenings throughout the spring and summer, out toward Thréig, watching for a low, square sail on the horizon that he knew would never come.

One September day, when the local corncrakes had all fled back to warmer climes, Father Martin was stepping off the coach from Cork. He was just returning home from a visit to his mother, when he saw a rough, dangerous looking stranger boarding the coach to Dublin. He only took note because the man was so young—surely not far from his own age—and men of his own age were not often seen in the village outside of major holidays. And usually those who did come never looked so dirty and weather-beaten

as this stranger did. He walked slowly to the priory, considering the wild, unkempt look of the man and the curious smile that nearly hid itself under his beard.

As Father Martin came up the stone path to his door, he was surprised to find a smooth green pebble on the stoop. He knelt to pick it up, turning it over and over in his fingers. A smile crept slowly across his face with the dawning of recognition. Pocketing the stone, he ran to the pier and shoved the blue and white rowboat out toward Thréig, digging at the waves with impatient oars.

When Father Martin approached the cottage on the cliff, his good shoes caked in black mud, all was still. There was no evidence of recent habitation, but all of the doors and windows of the cottage stood open to the air and the weather. Besides a pair of gulls that had wandered inside, there was no other sign of life there. The sheep shed, however, smelled strongly of tar and fresh black splatters dappled the dirt floor.

As he walked back into the kitchen garden, the young priest stopped at the rose bush where he'd buried the old fisherman's wife, a year ago to the day. He made the sign of the cross and knelt to see a small green pebble, like the one on his doorstep, nestled under the bush, and under it, weighed down by it, a mottled brown feather. He laughed as he stood, dusting the grass and dirt from his knees, and walked slowly back to his boat, shaking his head, quite unable to stop smiling.

As Father Martin rowed East back to the mainland and his flock, Seán rowed West and North. Far enough out from the rocks and reefs, he hauled his oars back into the currach and raised the sail. The *Corncrake* dipped and rose on the gentle, whispering waves. The old man reached a practiced hand into his left breast pocket and pulled out Muireann's white Easter glove, heavy now with tears of Saint Columcille. He kissed each fingertip and smiled before holding it out over the waves and letting it go. As it sank, the ghostly cormorant beat its black-feathered wings alongside the corn-crake at a respectful distance as she set out, once more, to sea.

www.ingramcontent.com/pod-product-compliance
Lightning Source LLC
Chambersburg PA
CBHW051139020726
47501CB00005B/1583

* 9 7 9 8 3 8 5 2 0 6 5 1 3 *

The Currach and the Corncrake